TALES FROM THE CURSED EDGE

DARK STORIES OF SWORDS AND SORCERY

MICHAEL MAGISTRO, JAMES ANDREWS, W.E. WERTENBERGER, ROB D. SMITH, JACK FINN, JP WILDER, CHRIS MASON

EDGE WEAVER LLC

Tales From the Cursed Edge
Dark Stories of Swords and Sorcery

Edge Weaver Realms is an imprint of Edge Weaver LLC

Copyright © 2025, Edge Weaver

Stories curated by Marie Ito.

Edited by JP Wilder, Bryn Reed and Marie Ito

Cover by: CBScout

Book Design: Marie Ito

Kindle ISBN: 978-1-964406-98-5

Paperback ISBN: 978-1-964406-99-2

Published in the United States of America

Edge Weaver LLC
19360 Rinaldi #681
Porter Ranch, CA 91326-1607

CONTENTS

THE SAVAGE RAT LORD
BY: MICHAEL MAGISTRO

Life Before Czar

Conner Andrus stood behind the greasy counter of Burger Barn, the din of the kitchen and the smell of burnt oil clogging his senses. The store clock inched toward closing time, but the order screen kept blinking, each new ticket more annoying than the last. The fry station hissed angrily, mirroring Conner's mood as he dumped another batch of fries into the vat.

"Last order of the night!" Carla shouted, tossing a damp towel over her shoulder. "I hope."

Conner rolled his eyes but forced a grin. "Better be, or I'm diving into the fryer."

Carla snorted, but he wasn't entirely joking. Every shift felt like an eternity—trapped in a loop of reheated burgers and nonstop complaints. Outside these fluorescent-lit walls, he was just a nineteen-year-old guy with a dead-end job and a fading dream of doing something that mattered. Something bigger than spatulas and timecards.

Sometimes, while scrubbing the flat-top or filling orders, he'd stare through the streaked front window and imagine being somewhere else. A battlefield, maybe. Or the deck of a spaceship. Anywhere but here, where his apron clung to him like defeat.

His thoughts drifted as he grabbed the trash bags and headed out the back. The alley was silent, save for the faint hum of the flickering dumpster light. He hated this part of the job. The stench of garbage mixed with the constant scratching from the shadows always put him on edge.

He hauled the first bag toward the dumpster when sudden movement made him freeze. A cluster of rats darted into the light, their bodies unnervingly large, their eyes glinting red.

"Gross," Conner muttered, edging around them. One of the rats hissed, baring its teeth. Conner stumbled back, nearly slipping.

"Okay, okay, you win," he said, dropping the trash and stepping away. But as he moved, his heel caught the edge of the dumpster. He fell backward, his head whipping toward the pavement—except the pavement wasn't there.

A swirl of purple and silver light consumed him. Weightless, he tumbled through a roaring void. He tried to scream, but no sound came. His chest burned as the world twisted and folded like a collapsing star.

Then—impact.

Arrival in Czar

He groaned, rolling onto his side. The ground beneath him was soft, damp, and cold. Definitely not asphalt.

The alley was gone.

Before him stretched a vast expanse of glowing hills beneath a massive pale-blue moon. The air was sharp, clean, tinged with a metallic tang. Strange trees with silver leaves swayed in the breeze, their trunks an iridescent black. The breeze brushed his skin like cool silk, tingling with electricity.

The sky above looked like a painted ceiling, speckled with stars that shimmered and danced. He could see two more moons in the distance—one green, one a deep crimson—hanging low on the horizon.

"What the ..."

Conner sat up, rubbing the back of his head. His uniform still reeked of grease, but everything around him was utterly alien. Dreamlike. But too vivid to be a dream.

He stood slowly, eyes scanning the surreal landscape. The air buzzed with distant insect chirps and strange calls—animalistic, yet musical. The ground beneath his feet was soft like moss, yet shimmered faintly with every step.

"Who goes there?"

He flinched at the sharp voice. A group of figures emerged from the shadows, armed with crude spears and axes. They were short—no taller than his chest—but stocky and muscular. Their braided hair framed sharp features, and their tight leather garb gleamed in the moon-light.

"Uh . . . hi?" Conner raised his hands slowly, unsure whether to run or stay put.

An older man stepped forward; lines etched deep into his face. "You are not of Czar," he said, gravel in his voice. "Yet you are no beast. Who are you, and why have you come here?"

"I don't know," Conner admitted, heart pounding. "I just . . . fell."

The man's gaze swept over him, lingering on his height. "Taller than our strongest warriors. Perhaps a gift from the gods—or a curse."

"I'm just a guy," Conner said, trying to steady his voice. "I don't want any trouble."

The villagers exchanged wary glances. At last, the elder nodded. "Come. If the night finds you here, you will not survive to see the dawn."

Life in the Village

The village of Arin was nestled in a quiet valley, ringed by steep hills and thick woods. Homes of stone and timber glowed softly with embedded crystals that pulsed in the night. Smoke curled lazily from chimneys, and the air was rich with the scent of burning wood and warm bread.

Conner was led to a modest hut near the center of the village, where a couple and their young daughter waited. The man was broad-shouldered and weathered, his face a study in stern lines. The woman had kind, welcoming eyes. Their daughter, no older than six, peeked shyly from behind her mother's skirt.

"We will house him," the woman said, her voice gentle but firm.

The elder nodded. "Very well. But watch him closely. If he brings misfortune, it will fall on your heads."

Inside, a small fire warmed the hut. The walls were adorned with woven tapestries, glowing softly in the firelight. Simple tools hung near the door, and dried herbs dangled from the ceiling beams.

The girl's curiosity soon overcame her shyness. She tugged at Conner's sleeve. "You're so tall! Are all your people giants?"

"Uh, no," he said, crouching slightly to fit beneath the low ceiling. "I'm just . . . average."

She giggled. Her parents remained serious.

"Listen carefully," her father said, voice low. "Do not go outside after dark. There are creatures here—monsters that hunt the night. If they find you, they will tear you apart."

Conner swallowed. "Got it. Stay inside."

And he meant it. But that didn't mean sleep came easily.

His mind raced. He tried to process everything—falling through a hole in reality, waking up on a different world, being called a gift or a curse by spear-wielding strangers. He lay on the edge of the straw mat, staring at the ceiling, where shadows danced like spirits.

Outside, the wind moaned through the trees.

He pulled the rough wool blanket tighter and told himself he'd figure it out tomorrow. Sleep tugged at his mind, dragging him toward uneasy dreams filled with shadows and silver leaves. Just before consciousness slipped away, a child's laugh jolted him awake.

The sound came again—high and carefree. Conner blinked, pushing himself up from the straw bedding. Through the small window, he caught movement in the moonlight. The little girl, her face bright with joy, chasing something across the village clearing. A ball, rolling toward the trees.

His stomach clenched. The father's warning echoed in his mind: *Do not go outside after dark.*

He was on his feet before he realized he'd moved, stumbling toward the door. The night air hit him like a slap, cold and sharp. The girl didn't see him, didn't hear his hissed warning. She kept running, closer to the tree line, closer to the darkness beyond.

And then the first shadow moved.

The Night of the Rats

A low growl rolled through the air, primal and deep. From the edge of the woods, a hulking form crept into the moonlight. It was massive—easily the size of a wild boar—with coarse, matted fur that glistened like oil. Its eyes glowed red, and rows of jagged yellow teeth caught the moonlight as it snarled.

Conner froze. His pulse spiked. Another shape emerged behind it. Then a third.

Three of them.

His breath caught as the creatures moved with unnerving grace, tails whipping behind them, claws digging into the frozen earth. Their gaze locked on the girl.

She hadn't seen them yet.

"Run!" Conner yelled, his voice tearing through the silence.

The girl turned, eyes wide with fear, but her legs didn't move. The closest rat lunged forward.

Conner bolted.

Every step felt like it took too long. The lantern swung wildly in his hand, casting twisted shadows across the trees. His boots pounded against the frozen dirt. He reached her just in time—scooping her into one arm and pivoting to place himself between her and the rats.

They stopped.

For a moment, all three rats crouched low, baring their teeth, their breath fogging in the cold air. Conner could feel the girl shaking in his arms.

"Stay behind me," he said. He set her down gently, positioning himself in front of her as the creatures began to spread out.

One to the left. One to the right. One straight ahead.

He spotted something out of the corner of his eye—a pitchfork leaning against a fence just twenty feet away.

Think fast.

He took a deep breath and ran for it.

The Battle

The rat in the center charged.

Conner lunged toward the tool, fingers outstretched. His hand closed around the wooden handle just as the rat slammed into him.

He twisted, using the creature's own momentum. With all his strength, he jammed the pitchfork forward, the prongs sinking deep into the rat's ribcage.

It screamed.

A hideous, high-pitched screech tore through the night as the rat writhed on the end of the fork. Conner pushed harder until the creature collapsed in a shuddering heap.

No time to breathe.

The second rat barreled into him from the side.

They both hit the ground hard. The lantern slipped from his grip and smashed, glass and oil spraying across the dirt. A flash of flame burst briefly, then fizzled out, plunging them into darkness.

Claws raked his left arm, slicing deep. He screamed in pain and kicked upward, catching the rat's belly and rolling free.

The pitchfork had broken in half during the fall.

He grabbed the jagged handle and spun just as the creature lunged again. With a snarl, he drove the broken shaft upward into its throat. The beast let out a gurgling cry, blood pouring down its chest. It twitched violently before crumpling.

Only one left.

The final rat paused at the edge of the trees, its eyes locked on Conner. Blood soaked the ground. Conner stood panting, shaking, one arm limp at his side. He met the creature's gaze.

A silent standoff.

Then, with a snarl, the rat turned and disappeared into the shadows.

The night held its breath.

And then it exhaled.

Conner dropped to one knee, the cold earth biting through the fabric of his pants. His lungs heaved like bellows, each breath ragged and sharp. His wounded arm throbbed in time with his heartbeat, blood trickling down to his fingertips. The broken shaft of the pitchfork slipped from his grip and fell to the ground with a dull thud.

His body trembled—not from the cold, but from the sudden flood of adrenaline wearing off. Every muscle in his frame screamed from exertion. His knuckles were raw, his side bruised from the impact of the second rat's charge.

He stared at the mangled bodies before him, barely recognizing them as anything from Earth. The stench of blood and burnt oil from the shattered lantern clung to the air, mixing into a nauseating fog.

The girl. Where was—

She stood behind him, motionless, her eyes glassy with shock. Conner reached out with his good arm and gently touched her shoulder.

"Hey . . . you're okay. It's over. I've got you."

His voice cracked. His throat was dry, and every word felt like gravel.

She blinked, then threw her arms around him, sobbing into his chest.

Conner let her cry. He held her tightly, his own tears stinging at the corners of his eyes. Not from pain, but from something else—some raw, unfamiliar mix of relief and horror and disbelief.

What just happened? What was he now?

Not a cashier. Not a fry cook.

He had killed.

Survived.

And in doing so, saved a life.

The Villagers Rally

A shout broke the silence—a man's voice, laced with alarm. Then another. Footsteps thudded against the earth as villagers spilled from their homes, drawn by the sounds of battle. Their torches flared in the night like tiny suns, pushing back the shadows.

Men and women armed with hoes, axes, and crude spears surrounded the scene. They took in the bodies of the slain rats. Blood pooled in the dirt. The air reeked of death and smoke.

One of the villagers pointed toward the woods. "There! It flees!"

A chorus of roars rose as a group of them gave chase into the darkness, their war cries echoing like thunder.

Conner stood slowly, cradling his injured arm. The little girl still clung to his side. Her parents rushed toward them—her mother falling to her knees, sweeping the child into her arms while her father's gaze locked with Conner's.

There were no words at first.

Only the silence of recognition.

Then, the father stepped forward and gripped Conner's uninjured shoulder.

"You saved her," he said, voice thick with emotion. "You saved my daughter."

Conner gave a slight nod, unsure what to say. He was lightheaded now, the pain in his arm intensifying. His legs felt like stone.

More villagers gathered. Their expressions shifted—from suspicion to awe, from fear to something else.

Respect.

They formed a circle around him. Whispers passed from person to person. Conner could feel their eyes on him—not as a stranger anymore, but as something more.

He had faced what they feared.

And won.

A burly man with a scar down his cheek stepped forward, eyes scanning Conner from head to toe. "No outsider would've done what you did," he muttered. "You didn't freeze. You didn't flee. You fought. Bled."

"The gods sent him," someone whispered.

"No," said an older woman with a bundle of herbs in her arms. Her voice was calm, certain. "The gods didn't send him. He came through something else. Something older. But he stood his ground. That is what matters."

"He saved the child!" cried a younger boy, no more than ten. "He fought those beasts like he was born to it!"

Conner shifted under the attention. He didn't know how to handle praise—let alone reverence.

A part of him wanted to disappear into the shadows again. Another part . . . felt something stir.

Not pride.

Belonging.

The crowd parted as the village elder approached, leaning heavily on his gnarled staff. The firelight reflected off the carved symbols etched into the wood. His face, a craggy map of wisdom and time, was solemn.

"Step forward, outsider," he said.

Conner hesitated, then obeyed.

The Naming Ritual

The elder's voice rose, clear and unwavering. "Tonight, something changed. We who have known fear, who have buried kin taken by the night, we saw it turned back. Not by blade or spell. But by the courage of one who did not owe us anything."

He turned to Conner. "What is your name, child of another world?"

"Conner John Arin Andrus," he answered quietly.

The elder nodded, then looked to the gathered crowd. "Too long. Too far. Names are not given freely in Czar—they are earned. Tonight, this one has earned his."

He stepped toward the body of the first rat, knelt, and dipped his fingers into its blood. Rising again, he faced Conner.

"From this night forward, you shall be known as Conner of Arin. Not as an outsider, but as one of us."

Conner stood tall as the elder raised his hand.

With a steady motion, the elder painted a line of blood down the center of Conner's forehead, then across each cheek—from ear to nose.

"The blood of your enemy marks you. The will of your heart binds you. You are no longer alone, Conner of Arin."

The villagers erupted into cheers. Where once they had turned away from him, now they reached out—hands clasping his arms, his back, clapping shoulders, speaking his name aloud.

And for the first time since arriving in this strange world, Conner believed it.

He was one of them.

The crowd didn't disperse. Not yet. They lingered, surrounding him not like a hero to be worshiped, but like a brother newly returned. Someone passed him a waterskin; another pressed a warm cloth to his wound. Hands were gentle but firm—familiar. The kind of touches meant for kin.

A young woman stepped forward with a bundle of cloth and a shy expression. "For your wound," she said, offering him a strip of clean linen.

He nodded, murmuring a quiet thank-you. She didn't wait for a response—just handed it to him and stepped back with a smile.

"We watched you fall from the stars," said a hunched man who smelled of smoke and iron. "We thought you were a warning. But maybe ... maybe you're a promise."

Children, previously silent, now inched closer. One of them reached up and touched the edge of Conner's tattered uniform. "Your skin armor is strange," the boy said. "But you fought like a warrior."

A ripple of laughter moved through the crowd.

Conner gave a half-smile. His limbs still ached, his arm screamed with pain, but in that moment, he felt lighter. Like something had been lifted from him—something heavy he hadn't even realized he carried.

And though the night had nearly taken him, it had also given him something in return.

A place.

A name.

A beginning.

A Warrior's Gift

Dawn crept over the hills in soft strokes of orange and gold, melting the frost from the rooftops. The village stirred with quiet energy, but for once, it wasn't rooted in fear.

Conner stirred from sleep, the stiffness in his limbs reminding him of every bruise and cut he'd earned the night before. His bandaged arm throbbed dully, but he welcomed the pain. It meant he was alive.

A sharp knock at the door interrupted his thoughts.

It swung open before he could respond. The little girl burst in, her smile wide and infectious. "Conner! Conner! Come! Mother and Father want to see you!"

He groaned as he swung his legs over the side of the cot. "Easy, kid. I'm still recovering."

"You're not allowed to rest. Heroes have to come when called," she said, grabbing his good hand and pulling.

Outside, the village was alive. People waved as he passed. Some bowed their heads. Others offered small nods of respect. The fear that once defined their expressions had been replaced by something else—hope.

At the edge of the village, the girl's parents stood waiting. Her mother sat on a low stool, a bundle of fur draped across her lap. Her father stood behind her, arms crossed and smiling—not just with approval, but pride.

"We worked through the night," her father said. "This is for you."

Her mother lifted the bundle, revealing a cloak made from the hide of the rat he had slain. The fur had been cleaned and stitched with care, lined with braided leather at the edges.

"All warriors of Czar wear the pelt of their first kill," she said softly. "It's tradition. And it's honor."

Conner reached out and touched the cloak. It was heavier than it looked, the coarse texture rough against his fingers—but it felt right. Earned.

They draped it over his shoulders, fastening the leather strap across his chest.

But the gift wasn't complete.

The father stepped forward again, this time holding something with both hands: a helm crafted from the skull of the rat. Hollowed, cleaned, polished. The teeth still gleamed beneath the rising sun.

He held it high, then lowered his voice. "This is the final rite. Bow your head."

Conner did.

The helm settled into place with surprising ease, its weight both grounding and empowering. It wasn't just a trophy—it was a symbol.

The father stepped back. "Rise, Conner of Arin. Whatever you were before, that life is gone. You are one of us now. You are a warrior."

Conner stood. The wind tugged at his new cloak. The villagers gathered once more, cheering not just out of gratitude, but recognition.

He wasn't just the outsider who fell from the stars.

He was their Savage Rat Lord.

And whatever lay beyond the hills—he would face it.

DENMÝR

BY: JAMES ANDREWS

What is this place?

How did I get here?

Darkness, pure and suffocating. A strange bubbling witch's brew of liquid flooded the ground beneath me. Rank gases and fumes threatened to stop my breath all at once.

Dead. That is what I must be. Finally defeated.

I attempted to move but the stinging, vile fluid surrounding me sucked my feet into the ground. I would have cut the horrid slime from my legs if only I could have found my sword.

"My sword, Denmýr! Where is it?"

Only when I reached into the muck for my sword did I realize how much the air had ravaged me. Breathing became agony, nose packed tight with noxious scum. My hands emerged, skin screaming as if I'd plunged them into a bubbling cauldron.

"Damn!" I snarled through the scalding hiss of my seared flesh.

"Hello! Hello! Hello!" my exclamation flittered bat-like into the stygian abyss, until a voice slithered out from the darkness.

"That will do you no good, Nadkrin, no good at all."

My heart slammed against my ribs as I spun toward the sound. Sweat beaded on my neck despite the chill. "Who goes there?" The words came out higher than I intended, betraying my fear. "Reveal yourself, coward!"

Far in the darkness, a pinprick of orange light bloomed like a distant star. The flame swayed with each step of its unseen bearer, casting writhing shadows that lay long across the mire's surface. As it drew closer, the light seemed to drink the darkness rather than dispel it.

"Ooh Nadkrin," the voice oozed honey-sweet poison, "poor, stupid king from the Ilithian mountains who thought he would follow in his

father's footsteps. What say you now, great warrior?"

"Bite thy tongue." I gritted my teeth and
hissed, "lest I carve it from your mouth."

"Tsk tsk tsk." The cloaked figure held the flame
aloft, its face hidden in shadows despite standing
a mere ten paces away. "Threats will not aid you
either. After all, *you* are the one who is trapped,
Nadkrin, I am free to move about as I please, do
you see?"

The flame flared white-hot, piercing the darkness like a miniature sun. Whether through magic or some other sorcery, I knew not, but in that
brutal light I saw them—corpses. Dozens, maybe
hundreds, of bodies sprawled in the muck, rotting in layers. Many had thrust their hands toward the ceiling in final, desperate pleas, frozen
forever in poses of supplication.

"Do you hear them Nadkrin? The screams of
the damned?"

I did hear them; the bellows of the dying
and tortured. Their screams reverberated in the
chamber—raw, animal sounds that assaulted my
ears. Some begged for mercy until their voices

cracked and failed, others just whimpered endlessly in the dark.

"Stop!" I shouted, holding my hands over my ears, "For the sake of the gods make it stop!"

The voices ceased. The flame went out, and I was plunged into darkness once again.

"A dream? A vision?"

"Not quite," said the voice.

The liquid seethed. Cold, rotting fingers clawed at my legs, then my waist, then my chest. The corpses surged upward, their putrid breath gagging me as melted flesh pressed against my armor. Their lidless eyes fixed on mine while strips of decayed skin sloughed off in my hands as I fought. I screamed a prayer to the Far Gates, but the undead pulled me deeper, deeper into their eternal grave.

That voice cut through the terror, "That'll do."

The dead slid back into the muck, leaving only the ripples to mark their attack. I gulped the air, grasping my chest for the sake of life itself. When the torchlight reappeared, the figure sat atop a stone, one leg crossed over the other, the torch held lazily in one hand. Through the shadow of her hood, I glimpsed a face weathered by centuries, skin drawn tight over ancient bones. Her white robe, now tattered and gray with age and decay, cascaded down to the filth beneath us.

"Witch."

She cackled; her mockery amplified in its hollow echo. "Witch . . . pff . . . don't insult me Nadkrin."

"Then what are you that you can stroll through this swamp and perform your tricks unmarred?"

"Tricks? Does this look like a trick?"

Light glinted off familiar runes as Denmýr emerged from the shadows behind her back, its massive blade singing through the air.

I gaped at her, my throat dry. "Impossible. Denmýr weighs as much as five fully grown men. No one but I can even lift—"

The woman's smile stretched wider. "Funny, isn't it? Nadkrin, the Wolf of Ilithia, so weak in this moment without his precious sword . . . what if I did this?"

With impossible grace, she flipped the great sword over, balancing its lethal point on her little finger. The blade—longer than she was tall—spun once, twice, dancing above her finger like a child's toy before settling back without even a tremor.

"This—this cannot be . . . The souls of my ancestors are bound to that blade—" My voice cracked with desperation.

"One thousand years of first-born sons," she cut in, trailing a finger along Denmýr's edge. "Each fallen warrior adding his soul, his weight, to this steel. Making sure only your bloodline could ever lift it into battle." Her smile turned cruel. "Such a predictable enchantment."

"You speak as if . . . but no. You're not from the mountains. You can't be one of my people."

"No, Nadkrin." She twirled the impossible weight of my family's legacy like a feather. "And like your ancestors before you, you're nothing but a blunt weapon."

"What do you mean, creature?"

"Swing the sword!" she pirouetted with Denmýr, her voice dripping to mock my ancestor's battle-fury. "Behead the wench! Take the village!" Each shout rang with generations of blood lust. She raised the blade high, her smile twisting. "Burn it down, burn it ALL down! Such simple creatures, you and your forefathers." She lowered the sword, contempt seeping from her words, "well . . . almost all of them. It's pathetic."

My jaw clenched until my teeth ached. How dare this withered husk mock my bloodline, generations of warriors who had carved our legacy into the mountains themselves? My fingers curled into fists in the muck, but I forced them to relax. I drew a slow breath, steadying my voice. Perhaps honey would work better than vinegar with this creature . . .

"Your opinion is noted, woman." I drew myself up as much as the muck would allow, summoning what dignity remained. "Now release me from this filth, return Denmýr to its rightful bearer, and grant me passage from this place."

Her laughter echoed off the walls, sharp as glass, "And what makes you think I'd want to?"

"If you didn't," I said, meeting her ancient gaze, "you'd have left me to rot with the others." I waved my hand at the charnel house that surrounded us.

The woman shrugged, tracing Denmýr's edge with one finger. "Perhaps, or perhaps I just want to torture you. You're familiar with the art, aren't you? Not just your enemies—innocent men, women, children—all who crossed paths with the great Wolf of Ilithia." Her lips curled. "How does it feel, Nadkrin? Being the prey. Being helpless?"

"I feel nothing but anger," I snarled. My voice echoed back at me from the cavern's walls. "And you'll taste its burning fury when I am free!"

"But you won't be free," she said, her sardonic smile widening. "Not without me. And you know it."

"Then tell me!" the shout tore from my throat. "I grow weary of this nonsense! Release me, tell me how to get out, or let me die. Your words don't torture me. They bore me."

"Shouting wastes precious air." She tapped Denmýr's blade against the stone. "This chamber is sealed. Each breath brings you closer to the end, no?"

I forced myself to breathe slowly through my nose, fighting back the urge to scream.

"Better." She nodded as if praising a child. "I will release you, but first, we must speak plainly of certain matters."

"My speech has been nothing but plain."

"Perhaps." Her ancient fingers traced patterns in the air. "But I suspect once I begin, you'll not only lie—you'll drown yourself in those lies."

"What lies?"

"You will see."

The hag rose from her perch, her feet leaving the stone, as if the earth's pull meant nothing. Blue light blazed in her eyes, making the flame beside her seem but a dying ember. Above us, azure flames roared to life, spiraling down until they formed a dome that trapped us in its strange glow.

"Observe, Nadkrin."

The dome rippled and I was assaulted with flashing images and drowning in sensation—the metallic taste of war, the stench of death, the very air thick with the weight of ancient battles. A thousand years peeled away like dead skin.

"Your ancestor, Dormiil, the Titan of Ilithia," her voice cut through the visions. "Watch how he claimed the western jungles from the serpent clans."

The flames swirled, revealing a vibrant western vine forest, its lush green canopy a stark contrast to its current desolate state; the heat shimmered above the scene. We followed a group of Ilithian warriors, their silver armor glinting faintly in the dim light as they crouched behind a fallen tree, swords and axes drawn, ready to strike. Beyond them, a column of serpent clan warriors slithered in formation. The serpents' lower bodies were like gigantic pythons, thick and scaled, but their upper bodies were unsettlingly human, with torsos and heads that looked almost normal. Among the serpent clan, women were of equal or even greater size than the men, creating a battalion of mixed genders identifiable only by the breastplates they wore. The immense King Sesroth headed the column, his spear a terrifying sight—four poisoned tips wickedly sharp, the shaft long and sinuous, ending in a ceremonial snake's head that seemed to hiss silently. Serpents wore Stanis-Gold armor, a metal surpassing even the strongest iron. Sesroth flared his nostrils, halting the march with a raised fist; his warriors reacted by readying their weapons.

From a treetop, Dormiil, my thousand-year great ancestor—a colossal Ilithian, far larger than myself—erupted in a rage, bellowing our clan's battle cry. In his hands he held Denmýr, poised to strike. He drove Denmýr into Sesroth's neck, dragging the blade down the length of the creature's body, severing the armor, skin, muscle, and bone with ease. That serpent blood would burn any normal man to death and gouts of it poured from Sesroth's body, splashing onto Dormiil's back, where it sizzled, smoked—and evaporated without leaving a mark.

Dormiil stood over the snake king's body and shouted for his men to attack.

I witnessed the carnage from the perspective of a terrified Ilithian private experiencing his first battle. In this boy's eyes, Dormiil appeared not so much a man, but rather a massive, rabid cave bear. More Ilithians poured from the tree line as Dormiil stood watching, a savage smile splitting his face. Then he dove into the carnage, Denmýr's blade rending serpent warriors to ribbons.

"Ten years," the woman said, her voice layered in a chorus of echoes. "That's how long Dormiil raged on."

I smiled, remembering Father's tales during our training sojourns in the Ilithian forests. "The serpents held out for a decade before surrendering. A glorious victory—Dormiil was a master of military strategy."

"But not of diplomacy, was he?"

"Diplomacy? I spat the word. "Those monsters would have fought to the last scale."

The woman sighed, "Witness . . ."

The scene shifted, a dizzying array of light and sound and smell. We'd left the jungles behind, entering the rocky hills encircling them. The horizon shocked me—where lush jungle had stood, only scorched stumps remained. Black clouds of ash shrouded the once-blue sky, turning day to twilight. We followed Dormiil and his warriors as they climbed the steep hill trail, until he suddenly halted, his keen eyes finding what others had missed.

"They're here, boys!" Dormiil's fist plunged into a rock crevice, emerging with a serpent warrior's tail. He yanked—the thirty-foot creature sailed through the air and crashed against the opposite cliff face. Before it could recover, Denmýr cleaved it in two. Dozens more serpent folk burst from their hiding places, slithering desperately up the trail. Dormiil thrust his blade skyward, and his men surged past him toward their prey.

"Ha!" Pride swelled in my chest. "Did you see that, woman? The strength! That creature weighed more than four cart oxen, yet Dormiil pulled it free as if plucking a splinter!"

She did not laugh. "Look closer," she commanded.

I did, and this time, when the scene replayed, my breath caught. The serpent had no warrior's tattoos, only the natural pattern of her scales. Though her head was shaved and her body massive, even for her kind, the covered breasts and delicate features beneath the blood and grime revealed the truth—this was no soldier but a young woman. Beautiful, even in death.

"It . . . it matters not . . . Those beast women are stronger than their men. She would have escaped, found a weapon, fought on. Any of them would have—"

The scene shifted, and through Dormiil's eyes, I watched our warriors pursue their prey up the hill. My words died in my throat. These serpents bore no warrior marks. The larger ones had breasts, flowing hair, faces that might have been called beautiful, if not for their terror. And the smaller ones . . .

"Children," the woman's voice cut through my denial. "They were children."

"You lie!" But my voice cracked. "Father never spoke of—" I steadied myself. "Even if they were. They would have grown to warriors themselves!"

"Your father did not tell you because he was unaware." Her words fell like stones. "Just as he did not know that the one to take up the throne after Sesroth's death, his son, Sanroth, met with Dormiil on peaceful grounds to surrender their lands. To give up the jungles to Ilithia."

"Once his people were chased into the hills, you mean?"

"No, right after Sesroth's death—ten years before they fled to the hills. Dormiil refused, of course."

Something twisted in my gut—Disgust? Disappointment? Shame? I pushed the feelings down. We are Ilithians! Our purpose is to conquer. To rule!

"I see your game, woman. Even if what you say is true, Dormiil was the king of Ilithia. Those lands were his to take from those slithering monsters if he chose to!"

"Fret not, Ilithian, there is much more I need to show you."

The scene dissolved into a marble city crowned with golden roofs, curved like a horseshoe around a vast lake. At its edge, the water plunged into an abyss so deep only mist marked where it met the earth. A single stone bridge extended from the main citadel, spanning the lake and stretching to the falls until it seemed to float in empty air. From our vantage point, it felt as if one were flying.

"Your great-great-grandfather, Olaquin the Reaper of Ilithia, spent nearly all his life attacking the golden city of Qin. Their wealth and access to vast gold deposits were great temptations to your ancestor, but what drove him to near madness was Qin's seemingly unnatural impenetrability."

Through Olaquin's eyes, we saw the golden city behind us, a landscape of crumbled stone and flame, the setting sun casting long shadows as black ash fell like snow. The Ilithian catapult missiles rained down fire, intense and searing, melting the golden roofs with their heat. The air was thick with the smell of molten metal. Qin people who tried to escape the structures were frozen in time as golden statues, forever writhing in agony from the liquid metal that encased their bodies. We stood at the end of the stone bridge, the rough texture cool beneath our feet. Ilithian soldiers, clad in dark armor, stood at attention along the sides; a line of chained people, their ragged clothes and weary steps echoing on the stone, marched closer.

A young woman, her face pale and her hands trembling violently, approached first; she was no warrior, soldier, or magic wielder. The cold iron of her chains fell away, and Olaquin propelled her to the end of the bridge, the wind whipping at her clothes as she stared at the distant horizon. Olaquin drew Denmýr from its sheath, placed the blade on the woman's neck, and, with a mighty heave, beheaded her where she stood. Her body tumbled over the falls, disappearing into the churning mist, the roar of the water deafening as the next victim, an old man, feeble and his eyes clouded with blindness, shuffled towards his doom. Just like the woman before him, the old man was beheaded and sent over the falls. The line moved, one after another, and Olaquin slayed each one in their turn. I watched each person die; the men, their faces contorted in agony, the women, their cries lost on the polluted air, the children, their eyes wide with terror, the servants, soldiers, concubines, maidens, princes, and princesses, all falling silently, one by one. The executions ran late into the night, and .
. .

"The blood falls of Qin . . ." My voice faltered. "Father and I saw them, but . . . in this vision the waters run blue. How?"

"You do not know their history, Nadkrin," The hag traced patterns in the air. "Those falls were Qin's shield, enchanted by the Warlock King Ganmar to preserve the city's peace for all time." Her fingers curled into a fist. "But even his magic couldn't withstand Olaquin and Denmýr. When the last soul in Qin was cast over the edge, the spell shattered. The waters run red with their blood even now and will until the end of time."

"Father told me Qin threatened Ilithia. Look at their wealth, their city—they could have raised an army ten times ours! My great-great-grandfather acted to survive."

"That is what your father told you, because that's what he was told."

"And why speak of Denmýr? Olaquin could have taken that city with a child's wooden axe, it was *he*, not the sword."

"Was it?" her ancient eyes fixed on mine. "Tell me, how strong do you feel without Denmýr in your hand?"

The truth of her words stung. With my sword so close yet unreachable, I felt hollow, weak. Madness crept at the edges of my mind.

"I can see you sweating, Nadkrin. Denmýr calls to you, it *needs* you by its side, lest its hold over you wane."

"Hold over me?" I fought to steady my voice. "I am the wielder of Denmýr. The sword's strength comes from the Ilithian chosen to wield it."

"How true." Her smile cut me to the quick. "Let me show you just how true that really is."

The blue fire swirled, and smoke filled my lungs. Each breath coated my throat with ash as I ran through the Valley of Flames. Curtains of volcanic debris parted before me, revealing enemies ahead. Beyond, the volcano fields painted the crimson sky with endless eruptions. Through the churning smoke, magic flashed like deadly rainbows—purple, green, red, blue, pink, white, yellow—each burst marking another clash in the hidden battle.

"This was your ancestor's complete subjugation of the wizarding guilds, their arcane libraries and laboratories reduced to ashes in the Valley of

Flames. They were but scholars who took pride in advancing the wizarding arts."

I became an Ilithian footman, and steel clashed around me as I charged through the chaos. A dark-robed wizard blocked my path, his staff blazing. Green fire roared toward my face—I felt its heat kiss my cheek as I twisted aside. My short sword flew from my hand, but the wizard knocked it away, answering with a streak of blue lightning. The bolt struck my left arm. Horror froze my breath as I watched my flesh crumble to dust in the wind.

Still I charged, leaping from the rocky wall to crash down upon him. The staff flew from his grasp. As he called it back with a chant, I snatched it from the air. Ancient Ilithian words burst from my throat, shattering the staff's protective magic. It splintered across my knee with a sound like breaking bones. The wizard's scream burst out as he spun, his body becoming a weapon to sweep my legs from under me.

I hit the ground hard. The wizard scrambled back, hands already weaving fire. No staff meant weaker magic, but his fingers and voice could still kill. My left arm was gone, my weapons lost—but an Ilithian is never truly disarmed. Ancient words burned in my throat as the wizard's hands blazed red. He clapped them together, unleashing a crimson pillar of death.

I twisted aside, catching his spell with a counter-charm. The red energy writhed, re-formed—became a spear of light twice my height. One spin, one leap, one throw. The spear took him through the heart, pinning him to the earth like a moth to parchment.

His mouth worked frantically, desperate for one last curse. My boot found his jaw. Teeth scattered like bloody pearls. His ruined tongue flopped uselessly as the light-spear finished its work.

"Brother!"

I turned. A white arc flashed.

Then . . . strange. I saw my legs fall one way, my torso another. The ground rushed up, dust and ash filling my mouth. Through dimming eyes, I saw my kinsman cut down my killer, then rush to where I lay scattered

"Eftin, by the gods!"

I coughed, blood leaking from my mouth, "we never should have been here."

My brother smiled at me, "No, Eftin, but no other choice was left us. At least we are together in the end. May we meet again past the Far Gates—"

His words were cut short by a searing beam of magic that ripped through his head, and he expired beside me.

Silence descended; no more spells crackled, no more wands glowed, only the retreating forms of wizards, their black robes swirling. The hands of my fellow Ilithians went up, raising their weapons in triumph. With a dramatic gesture, our king stood on a towering rock, his hand tracing Denmýr's path across the dark, malevolent sky.

"Charge, men! Into the volcanoes! Take prisoner whom you can but slaughter the rest!"

A flurry of feet pounded past me. The heavy boots sent a fresh wave of ash into my face, stinging my eyes as I looked up at the smoke-filled, burning sky, my brother's lifeless head heavy on my chest.

"None of us wished to be here, King Garindrol, you brought cattle to fight your war. May the Far Gates never grant you passage."

I squeezed my eyes shut, and the world dissolved into a velvety black, the last vestiges of light fading into the quiet darkness.

The smoke cleared from my lungs, the coppery tang of blood and the acrid bite of spent magic fading from my nostrils, but the screams and the carnage remained etched into my soul. A single tear, hot and salty, leaked from my eye.

I had not shed a tear since I was but a mere child.

"Garindrol . . . that was my father. That was his war against the wizarding cults."

"Not cults, Nadkrin, they were scholars. Your father was not threatened by their magical abilities. That was the lie he told you. The wizards were pacificists . . . And so, they were easy to conquer."

"Then, my father—"

"He kept only one in ten wizards alive to feed their power to Ilithia."

"Lies! I've ruled since I was seventeen. I have never seen a single wizarding slave."

"Oh, your father was thorough." Her smile twisted. "He buried them in their volcanoes, bound them with unbreakable spells of servitude and cursed immortality. Even now, they labor in darkness, their magic bleeding into Ilithia's bones. You've drunk their power all your life, never knowing the source."

" . . . Weak," said I, though softly, "the wizards were weak, and so deserve their subjugation, they . . . they . . . " but I could not finish the sentence. I kept hearing the boys' words, "never should have been here . . . cattle . . . never grant you passage."

The hag read my mind again, "Oh indeed, Nadkrin, you should have heard what your men said about you before you terminated their service in exchange for that undead army you summoned. Ah yes, those mindless, reincarnated souls ready to do Nadkrin the Wolf's bidding. Much more pliable than mere men, 'ey?"

"What did that soldier mean by no choice was left us?"

Her face darkened, "If they did not want to fight, what then?"

"They didn't look like soldiers. Not like the men I trained. Their occupations must have been artisans or money counters, if they did not want to fight, they had but to remain in their professions."

"That was the choice you offered when you became king. Garindrol was not so fastidious. Your father conscripted every man to take up arms against the wizards, even boys as young and weak as those two."

"Then why didn't they simply leave Ilithia? Our walls are not sealed, people are free to go whenever they wish."

"Go where? Do you truly think the world respects the kingdom of Ilithia or its people? That they give you their coin to fight more battles, their women to breed more Ilithians, or their children to mold into more soldiers out of admiration? No, Ilithians are hated amongst the rest of mankind. You are the king, you were once the prince, your exposure to the world has been occluded by the veil of royalty and power until the day Denmýr came into your possession and completed your corruption as it did your father, and your father's father, and on and on."

"Corruption?"

The woman remained silent, her hands a blur as the blue flames surrounding us shifted, glowing with a tranquil, verdant green. Sitting on a grassy hill in Ilithia, the warm sun on my face, I etched scenes of battle into the soft, yielding dirt with the tip of my short sword. The pounding of hoofbeats drew my attention to a group of men on horseback riding towards me, my father at their lead.

Leaning against the tree opposite me, an Ilithian shield caught the morning light, its polished surface reflecting my face—MY face—with startling clarity. The day my father left to conquer the dwarf kingdoms in the center continent was carved into my memory; I was sixteen, and the weight of this day felt heavier than any mountain.

"Son, why do you tarry outside the walls?"

He was a giant. At sixteen, I was unusually tall, towering over most men, but my father, astride his horse, seemed to reach the very treetops.

Denmýr was secured on his back.

"I came to bid you farewell, father and wish you strong winds and a stronger arm. I only wish that I could accompany you."

Father smiled and tousled my hair with his gloved hand.

"The last campaign you joined me on was too close a call. Your mother would have hanged me from the nearest tree had you come back in any worse condition."

A shared chuckle erupted from us and the officers.

"You need not worry about me, son. I will secure new lands for you to rule when the throne is yours. Raise a salute for me, Nadkrin."

I paid my respects to Father in the Ilithian manner: sword beside my head, blade down, a slight bow. Then, his hand steadfast, Father did something he had never done before: he drew his dagger and saluted back, prompting the officers on their horses to salute me as well.

The happiest moment of my life.

I watched Father and his men descend the hill, their shadows stretching like dark fingers across the trail. Beyond, masses of Ilithian war-riors turned the green fields black, a sea of ar-mor and steel that stretched to the horizon. In the air hung the weight of destiny, as heavy as storm clouds before rain. Messenger hawks soared overhead, cutting dark shapes against the sun as they winged back toward the city. I squint-ed against the harsh light, watching them fade into the glare as if they'd flown past the Far Gates themselves.

The scene changed once more; I was a year older, the moon hung heavy in the inky sky, slaying the darkness, and a chilling wind whis-pered through the trees. Father had trained me to maintain heightened awareness even in sleep, so I heard the messenger hawk's wings beat-ing, a distinct sound, long before it neared the palace. Heart pounding, I raced to the balcony and caught sight of the bird, its feathers ruf-fled and bloody, somehow still beating its wings and holding flight. I recognized Ces, a hawk with feathers the color of burnt umber, one of six royal messengers. A light flickered on in the cham-bers next to mine. On the terrace beside me, my mother emerged, squinting in the dim light, unable to identify the bird.

"That's Ces!" I said, "he is badly hurt, he—"

"By the gods!" Mother's cry pierced the morning. I turned to see Ces plummet from the sky, a broken arrow against midnight. I burst from my bed chambers, flying ahead of my mother down the stairs. Guards formed a circle around the messenger's crumpled form, snapping to attention as I approached. I had grown much since the previous year and I towered over them now, even barefoot against their boots—no longer the boy they'd known.

Ces' head lolled in my palm, neck splintered like dry straw. I offered a final salute before my eyes found the message—scorched parchment tied to his leg with twine.

The king is dead. The dwarven armies have enlisted the aid of night creatures in multiple surprise attacks on our battalions. We are making a full retreat. All hail King Nadkrin, son of Garindrol.

Mother reached me as the words burned in my mind.

I passed the note to Mother without meeting her eyes. She drew in a deep breath. Neither of us wept—Father had taught us tears were weakness.

She gripped my shoulder, pulling me to my feet. "King Garindrol is dead," she announced to the gathered guards. Her voice never wavered. "My son, Nadkrin, is your new King."

The guards sank to one knee in unison, their swords laid beside their bowed heads in the ancient gesture of fealty.

"Rise." Mother's command cut through their silence. "No one breathes a word of this until morning. We'll present Ilithia's new king after the sun rises."

As my mother was wont to do, she pulled me in, arms on my shoulders. Her dark eyes, intense, determined, met mine. "I will miss your father dearly, as you will, but he died valiantly. He trained you well. You will make a great king."

She kissed my cheek, then went to bed.

Sleep took me like a murderer—dreamless, still as death. Dawn's first light crept across my chamber floor, broken by an unfamiliar shadow.

There, against the balcony rail, Denmýr waited.

I rose, each step drawing me toward my birthright. The moment my fingers closed around its hilt, power surged through my veins—not just strength, but something darker, primal. A storm of confidence and fury boiled in my blood. I drew the blade, its ancient steel singing, and raised my ancestors' legacy to the sky.

Pride in my crown, grief for my father—these thoughts never came. Only rage filled me, pure and savage. I would hunt the dwarves who killed my father. I would tear apart their night-creature allies. My hand, now wielding Denmýr's might, would reach beyond Ilithia's borders and crush all who stood before me.

My first morning as king of Ilithia.

Surrounding us, the fiery blue vortex cycled through many scenes, benign and malignant. Two years after claiming my crown, I left my bride and infant son to hunt my father's killers. But

Denmýr's thirst wasn't slaked by dwarven blood and night creatures. We marched west, to the colossal silver mines where peaceful dwarves had never raised a hand against us. Their halls ran red. Still, we pressed on to the shores where sea-folk cities crumbled at our arrival.

When we took to ships, sailing toward the unknown lands, my men's spirits broke. Let them break. I abandoned them to seek the fabled magic plains—where the Far Gates' power ran thick as honey, where even my meager magic could become legendary. There, I raised an army of the dead and gave my kinsmen their choice: fight beside us or feed my new legion, for cowards would find no welcome in Ilithia's halls.

Many Ilithian warriors refused my offer. They were swiftly dealt with by the relentless undead. I surveyed the scene of carnage my reanimated horde exacted upon the traitorous Ilithians with Denmýr by my side. They were my people, and still, I was glad of the sight.

But now, trapped in this cavern with the hag and her blue flames, I longed to weep for the kinsmen I had murdered.

"Now we come to the ultimate vision," she hissed.

The scene shifted to the battle I'd just waged before I woke up in the darkness. I led my army toward a gleaming white city that had haunted my dreams. Looking back, I saw that there were no more Ilithian kinsmen left among the ranks, only a sea of undead slaves. Boulders rained down from the city's catapults, crushing my soldiers to dust, but I was too swift for their aim. We swarmed the walls like insects, and I fixed my gaze on the highest tower where surely their king awaited.

But at the tower's peak, no guards met me. Instead, a white dragon reared up, its wings creating storms with each beat. I leaped onto its armored side, Denmýr finding purchase between scales as I climbed. My blade pierced its sapphire eye, sheared off a horn.

The beast thrashed, but I clawed my way to where its heart must lie. My fingers dug into iron flesh as Denmýr plunged deep—a killing blow. The dragon's roar shook the heavens as it flung me loose. Before I could right myself, massive jaws snapped shut around my leg. The world spun as it hurled me skyward. Denmýr slipped from my grasp.

Then darkness, as the dragon's throat swallowed us both. I slammed against fleshy walls until consciousness fled.

"Then I woke up here," I said.

The swirling blue fire overhead disappeared, and the hag returned to the rock, holding the torch out with her hand.

"I am in the belly of the beast?"

She nodded.

"Then, what . . . what are you?"

"I am Renala, the white dragon. When Denmýr pierced my heart, I knew my fight was over. After swallowing you, I retreated into my spirit form to meet you. Denmýr's attack was fatal, but I have just enough time to make you see reason."

"Dragon, I . . . I don't understand what is happening to me. That rage that has defined my life is fading, but I want to cling to it as desperately as a drowning man grasps for a shore."

"Denmýr does this, Ilithian. As a boy, ancestral words infected you; as a man, it is the blade preserving your legacy that poisons you."

"Denmýr isn't poison . . . it isn't, it can't be. It is all I've ever known."

"What do you think Denmýr really is?"

"My family's sacred sword, passed down for a thousand years and imbued with the souls of all its former wielders."

The dragon spirit shook her head, "Not quite. That is the story that survives today, but your lineage extends much farther than a mere millennium. The first of your line to wield the sword, Ara, was the founder of Ilithia over ten thousand years ago."

"Impossible, how do you know this?"

"I am old Nadkrin, far older than you care to surmise. I was young when Ilithia was a mountain hideaway for refugees from an ancient slave state. Your ancestor led these runaways, hoping to escape by fleeing into the mountains. However, their pursuers followed and trapped them on Gathril's peak. During combat, Ara was thrown down the mountain and almost killed . . . It just so happens that one of my kind lived on that mountain as well."

"A dragon?"

"There were many more of us before the wasting disease wrought its devastating fury. Ensanor, the black dragon, responded to Ara's calls to the Far Gates and offered him Denmýr, a weapon made from Gathril's stone walls. Ensanor restored Ara's strength to defeat his enemies and assured him that Denmýr would provide unimaginable power, which would be inherited by his descendants indefinitely."

"And their souls would bless the blade upon their deaths!" I shouted, staring like an awe-struck child at this new telling of my family history.

The dragon spirit shook her head again, "Not blessed, not imbued . . . imprisoned."

"Imprisoned?"

"Every wielder's soul is trapped within Denmýr, unable to escape. When you take innocent life, Nadkrin, those souls feel the agony. You heard their screams once, not long ago."

"By the gods . . . the pleas from these corpses
. . ."

"Not their screams—the wails of those bound
to Denmýr. Your father, his father, backwards
through time. Forever."

The truth struck me mute.

"Can you not see, Nadkrin? Ara used Denmýr
for justice, to free your people from chains. But
power corrupts. Each wielder craved more, took
more, until we come to you—the Wolf of Ilithia.
The worst scourge this world has ever known.
The one who will bring about Its destruction."

"No . . . I'm not . . ." But the words died in my
throat.

"I speak the truth, boy. Even now, your army
of dead things claws at my dying flesh, trying to
free you. You would have led them to devour the
world had I not trapped you here."

"So, my family line is doomed. Is that what you
say? You mean we are cursed to remain villains
forever, like those Ara fought—until the world's
destruction?

"That's right. The loudest screaming in that
blade is from Ara himself, who has had to live

these ten thousand years watching his lineage fall to the level of his enslavers."

"Then I will cease my campaign. I will recall my undead army and disperse Ilithia's legions until we are scattered to the winds!"

"That is not enough, Nadkrin."

"Not enough? What more can be done?"

"Ilithian, I believe that something past the Far Gates brought us together for a reason, so that I may help you in breaking your family's curse."

"Please, Dragon—grant me an enchantment or a wish, as Ensanor did for Ara."

"Ensanor cursed your family. I offer something greater: a quest."

"A quest?"

Her ancient eyes burned into mine. "Rectifying your sins alone is not enough for purification. Your bloodline's blight stretches beyond horizon's edge, and your ancestors writhe in Denmýr's grip, trapped by Ensanor's curse."

"What would you have me do?"

"The quest I grant upon you is this: Go forth and right the wrongs of all five hundred ancestral souls within that blade; as you repair each soul's misdeeds, the blade will become lighter.

The dragon spirit drew forth a crimson feather that glowed like ember-light, as long as a dagger. "The last Great Phoenix presented a feather to ten chosen friends before his final burning. I was one of them." She placed it in my hands. "When Denmýr balances on this feather as easily as I balanced it on my little finger, your quest is complete. The curse breaks, and you will be free to forge your own path from then on."

"If I fail?"

"Should you fail, it would ensure the world's destruction. Denmýr will return to your son in Ilithia, and I will not be alive to aid him as I am currently aiding you."

I tied the feather along a chorded rope of my hair.

"Then I will not fail you, Renala."

"Go now. No longer the Wolf—I name you Phoenix of Ilithia. Right these ancient wrongs, restore balance, and do with Denmýr what you do best." She waved the sword, then held it in her open palm. She said, "Your hand . . ."

I extended my hand. Denmýr flew to my grip without spell or incantation, but something had changed. The familiar rage felt muted, distant—the curse already weakening. The leather creaked beneath my fingers, an old friend speaking new words.

"Listen." Her voice dropped lower. "Your ghouls await, hungry for their master's command."

The moaning and cries of the undead horde howled around us.

"My task is complete. Fly, Phoenix of Ilithia. May we meet again someday, past the Far Gates."

The spirit and its flame disappeared, leaving me in the silent innards of the beast.

The phoenix feather blazed behind my ear, casting shadows in the dragon's gut. One swift cut freed my ankles from the bile.

I pressed my palm to the stomach wall, drew a deep breath, and raised Denmýr before me. The blade sang through the air, parting dragon-flesh like spring ice. Light flooded in, blinding but pure. Below, my undead legion waited, weapons raised to welcome their master's return.

I bellowed my family's war cry—not in conquest now, but in redemption. As I leaped from the dragon's body, I watched the triumph drain from their rotting faces, replaced by terror.

Denmýr's edge caught the dawn as it fell toward undead flesh. And so my quest began.

THE MANY MOUTHS OF THE ENDLESS NIGHT

BY: W.E. WERTENBERGER & ROB D. SMITH

Kayson fought to keep his footing on the brine-slick stone walkway in the Butcher's District of Ullshak, City of a Thousand Sails. It didn't help that he and his two compatriots had just left their third tavern of the night in this raucous city on the edge of the Taman Sea. They had filched a wine pot at the last bar to keep them warm on the streets. A storm brewed in this city of scoundrels and whores. The clouds shrouded the dark deeds that transpired on her streets, and the rain could do little to wash away the debauchery.

Kayson, Makari, and Delarus deserved to prowl this town spilling the tale of their latest adventure for Baron Munro of Calaxis. They helped him secure a book of lineage from his cousin across the neighboring land. The fool thought he could have his scribes rewrite the pecking order and eliminate his competition for land and crown with ink instead of blood. Blood would always be the first choice of leverage in this forsaken world. The trio along with a few other sworn men besieged the cousin's keep and took the book by force, earning them welcome heft to their collective purse. Kayson and his friends weren't ones to save for some fertile farmland and a plump wife to tend to them in their dotage. Nay, they would retire from their mercenary ways when their heads were severed. Until then they fought hard and caroused just as heartily.

In this broken town, you couldn't leave your weapons in the room you rented. When you stepped out at night, you did so with your sword or axe nestled close. You never knew when negotiations for dancing with another man's woman would turn aggressive. So far none had tested the mettle of his trio, none save for this potent wine. It kicked like a cart mule. Kayson stumbled and Delarus couldn't keep his stream of piss straight on the wall he aimed at.

"Makari, for 'Fate's sake man, help our friend in need. He's sprung a leak."

"Aye, hold this." Makari handed the wine pot and went over to their urinating friend. He placed a boot on his backside that shoved Delarus closer to the wall. The piss back splashed, and he roared.

Kayson laughed so hard that he spilled some wine. He turned his back on his friends and lapped up more of the libation. It was while drinking that he heard Makari shout and a squeak in response. He spun drunkenly around to find his bearded compatriot holding a slim child wrapped in grey bedraggled clothing by the collar. The child's face was so covered in soot and ash that he couldn't tell if it was a boy or a girl. Furious eyes popped against the blackness of their cheeks with a glint of purple. The gaze seemed oddly familiar.

Dangling from the child's finger was a slim funneled spike. The strong wine had robbed Kayson of his senses, but the recognition of an urchin in distress ran deep within his scarred soul. That was the same look his sister Tayla had when they crawled the gutters of their town. Orphans from a shallow little fiefdom skirmish, too small to be called a battle but large enough to flatten their way of life. He hadn't thought of his sister in ages since he abandoned her to the mercy of the streets. Until he stared into those familiar hungry eyes.

"Cut me while trying to open my pocket for coin, you little bug." Makari shook him like a rat. "Drop your jabby spur!"

The street urchin swung his hollow spike at the arm that held him. Makari dropped him and roughly put his boot in the urchin's hind side. The child skidded into a roll across the cobblestone. Kayson flinched but refrained from calling out his distaste. No worse for wear, the little street rat stood up brandishing his spike. There was a bit of blood on the tip of it. The urchin brought it to his sooty lips and flicked out his tongue for a taste. Kayson's stomach lurched, not at the act but at the pleasure that came over the gutter child's face at the taste of his friend's blood.

"I'll clean up the wee devil." Delarus of the endless bladder turned mid-piss, showering the child in a yellow sea. Makari bellowed a laugh so loud it echoed off the alley walls. A rat scrambled out of the urchin's shabby garments, shook its dark fur, and took a defensive posture on his shoulder. The waif wiped his face clear, and angry purple eyes blazed behind his fingers.

The street urchin whispered to the rat. The vermin swung its head at each member of the trio, but its beady eyes stopped on Delarus. The grimy urchin stabbed repeatedly in the air towards him. Delarus wobbled back on wine-addled legs. The rat ran down the child's leg, and if a rat could roar like a speckled jungle tiger, that's what it did: a high-pitched roar. Tiny unseen movements made the hair on Kayson's arm rise. Rats skittered out of the shadows, forming a cadre around the urchin. There must have been over fifty vermin at its feet. The little thief uttered what could only be called a curse, and then spit at Delarus' feet. One last stab of his hollow spike, and the urchin scrambled toward the deep shadows of the alley. When he was safely away, his rat defenders followed him like the Pied Piper of the tall tales.

Kayson found he had drawn his blade. Barktown. That was the name of his hometown. The unholy urchin had driven up lost memories. Ill memories. He laughed, hoping to mask his distress from his companions.

"That's a lesson he won't soon forget," Delarus said, giving one last shake before tucking himself away.

"Or she."

"Or it." Makari shivered, then waved for Kayson to hand over the wine pot.

"Could well have been a she. Hard to tell at that age," Kayson said, passing the pot.

"No matter. May the next plague that sweeps this wicked city take that demon child and his disease-spreading vermin back to Hades." The brawny warrior drained what remained of the wine, dashing the clay pot against the same wall

Delarus had just marked. "This way. I know of a little place on the next corner. The drink is swill, but the serving wenches are fetching."

Kayson shrugged; his sword-brother laid out their creed succinctly. Life was borrowed and best lived fast. Better to leave the past where it lies. If he had stayed behind with his sister, they both would have been ravaged by the gutters. There was a single chance for one of them to escape. He grasped it before she could. He ran to catch up with his friends, joining them in a bawdy refrain of "The Merchant's Wayward Wife."

Not one of them witnessed the multiple pairs of ravenous eyes watching from the dark gutters.

*

"Open! By the authority of the Tri-Council."

Kayson shot upright, spitting straw and trying to untangle himself from his sleeping companions. The redheaded lass cursed his parentage while the brunette woman continued snoring.

"Open this door." The order was repeated, followed by a loud banging.

"Whoever that is, tell them to sod off," Makari growled from across the room. His mat of straw was occupied by another dark-haired woman.

Kayson found his underclothes and did his best to climb into them. His head felt three sizes too big, and his stomach heaved. He reached the door just as the banging began again.

A yawn was all he managed as he flung the door wide. Standing before him was a city guardsman wearing spit-shined chain mail armor and holding a cudgel. Behind him stood the two biggest men in armor Kayson had ever witnessed. There shouldn't be enough chain in all of Ullshak to cover these two bastards, but here they were.

"Everyone out, by authority of the council," the man said.

"What did we do?"

"You lot are coming with me to Lady Miva's establishment."

Kayson detested dealing with heel-lickers. "Kind of tony calling a brothel an establishment."

"Gather your garments or walk naked across the city with your nobs hanging. It makes me no never mind."

Makari came to the door naked except for the scars kissing his hairy frame. Kayson noticed a fresh crescent-shaped gouge on his lower hip. "Get bent. Some coin went into the magistrate's pockets our first day here."

"Such tithing allows you latitude for frivolity in Ullshak, but things can go too far. Now dress and heed my words. You are going to Lady Miva's for rectification." The lackey backed up until he stood between his two guardsmen.

Kayson was too spent from the last night's revelry to scrap with these oafs. Best to sober up first. Lady Miva was very hospitable, but perhaps she was miffed they took a couple of her earners home with them.

He leaned to his naked friend. "Wake Delarus if you can. It seems we have a stroll to take."

Makari belched but thankfully blew it away from him. "I saw when I rose that the lout's bed is empty. He's not here."

"Damn his hide. He stayed all night at Lady Miva's, didn't he? The worthless bastard must have been too sotted to walk."

"I'm not here to debate the merits of your friend. Heed my call or these two will drag you." He tapped his cudgel on his two goons' armored chests. All those two did was exhale fetid breath in tandem.

As they made their way to a pile of clothes, Kayson pointed at Makari's hip. "Is that where that little thief nicked you aiming for your coin purse?"

"Aye, it hurts worse than getting sliced by a halberd." Makari touched the cut. "Warm to the touch."

"The imp's foul spike may have carried disease. After we collect Delarus, we'll take you to a cunning man for some salve. Can't have an infection from an alley leech take down the mighty Makari."

"Indeed," yawned Makari.

Kayson and Makari flung some clothing together, rallied the women to get dressed as well then went out into the midday of the City of a Thousand Sails. The demon sun had decided to poke its eye out from behind the storm clouds. The one day a hungover warrior could have used the shade from the clouds was now. Kayson didn't think they were cursed, but here they were trailing a heel-licking government lackey instead of sleeping nestled next to soft bosoms.

"I'm going to strangle the fat wretch."

Makari mouthed foul sentiments toward Delarus as well. Insults wouldn't be enough. They would have to fine him, three coppers apiece for his infraction. Kayson laughed at their arrangement. They always fined each other for fool's moves that hindered their lives in some fashion. It was Delarus himself who had devised their self-governance during one extended lull in battle. The trio had voted unanimously for their common good, but because it only took two votes to fine someone and the two voters got the coin, the made-up justifications to fine got out of hand.

Makari, reading his mind, said, "Three coppers apiece."

Kayson laughed. "We may need all our coin to fix what our brother has broken. This lawless city cares not about the chaos you unleash as long as you pay your fair share in tithes. I can't imagine what he's gotten himself into."

"He wasn't there long enough to impregnate someone, even if he could get his serpent up."

One of the women from last night pushed past them. "He better not have burned the place down. I have nowhere else to go."

Kayson sniffed. The stench of the city was certainly strong enough to mask the scent of a fire, but as he looked in the general direction of Lady Miva's he didn't see any smoke climbing to join the clouds. Bless the Fates for that. At least their friend hadn't burned the place to ashes with his pipe. The unmerry duo trounced all the way there with aching heads and unanswered questions about Delarus.

*

"That big ogre was dead at my front door when we found him," Miva said with a sweep of her arms toward their unmoving friend lying belly up. "There was this pounding that almost knocked my door down followed by wailing. 'Get off! Get off! Get them off!'"

Kayson looked at the heavy oak door, stout enough to protect the women inside. Eight long gouge marks were trailing down wood. Delarus, the third of his name and heir to nothing, laid before them, broken fingernails on the tip of every finger. His face was frozen in a mask of fear that Kayson had never witnessed in any bloody skirmish. The lackey was down on one knee examining the remains.

"All the clamoring from the brute ran most of my customers out the back. Everyone thought the hordes were coming, but it was only this dead behemoth blocking my door. Much coin was lost."

"Witch! You talk of lost coin. That's our fallen brother!" The lackey's guards had barely managed to grab Makari as he lunged toward the madam. Thank the Fates for small favors; he would have throttled the woman.

"Take him inside to cool off," the lackey ordered.

The guards did so, but they would have had an easier time if asked to drag away a horned drang from its egg clutch. Just a few moments before both Makari and Kayson had sworn bodily harm upon their besotted compatriot. Now Kayson was ready to slay anyone for dishonoring his corpse.

"Bit by the little demons." This came from the lackey, drawing Kayson's attention away from the inconsolable Makari.

"What?"

He used his cudgel to point at Delarus. "Those marks."

Kayson saw them now. Bloody holes were torn into the linen fabric of the man's trousers.

"Vermin did this." It wasn't a question.

Kayson had to know. He yanked down his dead compatriot's trouser legs. His legs were covered in countless marks, brothers to the mark that was on Makari's upper thigh. The filthy urchin's spike.

The lackey nodded, knowingly. "Perhaps. Wouldn't be the first man to fall asleep on the street and wake up with a rat bite or two."

Kayson never liked rats. Wharf rats were gargantuan, but there was something about gutter rats that gave him the shivers. How they moved in a choreographed swarm as if of one mind. He recalled that time he and his sister Tayla were hiding from an orphan master collecting wayward children. They had squeezed themselves through a small opening in the drop chute and taken refuge inside a grain storehouse, A pungent uric odor permeated the room. It conflicted with the earthy fragrance of the grain-filled bags.

Tayla curled her lip at the pervasive smell but they had time to find a better hiding spot. He put a reassuring arm around her. keeping deathly quiet until the bags they sat on began to squirm. His sister jumped away first. He bit down a scream when the first rat crawled out of the bag and across him. Bit down so hard he drew blood from his cheek. The nasty smell had been rats. Neither one could stop screaming when hundreds of rats surged out. Sharp tiny claws crawled over him.

"But we both know rats didn't do this. Not alone," said the lackey.

"Have you seen such marks before?"

"Similar, aye. Your fat friend isn't the only strange death in the Butcher's District. They say not to walk alone during the devil's hour." The lackey got to his feet. He leaned close to Kayson and spoke in a hushed tone. "I suggest you and your angry compatriot depart the city."

"And if we don't leave?" Kayson's blood was up.

The lackey gave a nod to Delarus' body. "Then I expect to find you both in the same sorry condition. That's not a threat; that's a near certainty. There have been a lot of bodies lately."

The last of his patience spent, Kayson grabbed the man's elbow and jerked him close. An officious toad the man may have been, but to his credit, he didn't blanch when confronted. "Speak plain and speak fast."

The lackey pulled his arm free and looked around before he uttered, "You had a run-in with a cutpurse last night, yes?"

Kayson nodded.

"A child, dressed in rags, possessing a dark visage with luminous eyes?"

"We did," Kayson said. "A wee creepy one had a go for Makari's purse. We shook some sense into the urchin and sent it away."

The lackey shook his head slowly. "That little demon killed your friend, and it wasn't alone."

"Demon spawn." Kayson rolled those words across his tongue.

The lackey stamped his cudgel on the stone. "The official position of the Tri-Council is there are no wicked creatures inside the city walls besides the occasional rat. The common folk can put up with the odd vermin nicking their wares. But there are whispers of other vile entities."

"I assume whispers are costly?" Kayson dug into his coin purse for a few coppers. He held them low but clinked them together for the lackey to see.

The lackey held his hand below the coins and craned his head to see if anyone was watching. No sooner than the coin touched the skin of his palm did he make them disappear into his purse. "There is a blight at the heart of the city. These attacks are only a symptom. You're just another blowfly being drawn to the smell of a dying carcass."

Kayson despised being fooled after his coin had been spent. "Out with it, watchman. Where do these wretched creatures hide? Where is their den?"

The lackey shrugged noncommittally. "My guess would be the Tumbledown. Been abandoned for ages, and it's prone to flooding. Even the beggars can't find purchase amidst such foul ruins."

Kayson nodded. "Any other counsel on these affairs?"

"Best go in with full kit, sell sword," the lackey said in parting. "Small in stature they may be, but even ants working together can strip a drang's carcass to the bone."

*

After agreeing on a sum to cover the burial of Delarus, Kayson left the brothel to find Makari. He was sitting on a curb, his face in his hands. In all the skirmishes they had fought, in all the horror they had seen and taken part in, he had never seen his sworn brother weep.

"I took care of the arrangements," Kayson said sitting down next to his only remaining friend.

Makari rubbed his eyes and nodded. "Tell me you didn't pay off that hag too."

"No. We agreed that Delarus' empty purse more than made up for the loss of business. The madam feigned ignorance but didn't press the issue any further."

Makari coughed out a laugh. "He always did overpay for company and wine. Guess that coin was destined for the brothel's coffers one way or another."

"Aye." Kayson produced a wineskin and threw back a slug, then passed it over.

"Our Delarus," Makari said and raised the wineskin to the skies before wetting his lips. "What now?"

"We do what we've always done. We take a count. Who's in favor of tracking down whatever killed our friend?" He raised his hand.

Makari slammed the empty wineskin to the stone-lined walk and shouted, "Aye."

Kayson clasped him roughly around the neck and brought him close. "We could always use these two votes to penalize Delarus' ghost."

"Nay, let's put fire to this city until the murderer comes forth."

"Sounds like our regular strategy. Create a ruckus and proffer." Kayson slapped his friend between his shoulder blades, wishing for another full wineskin or pot because he did not feel as courageous as his words. The city of Ullshak had taken a stalwart friend and brought back childhood unease. Evil was soaked into every stone-cobbled vein of this place. He could feel it leaking out and infecting all around him. The very air was foul.

Such an evil was why he ran away from his birthplace, scampered away from the responsibility of his sister Tayla. Men, women, and even other alley waifs beset upon Kayson and his sister, taking liberties and advantages of them at their weakest. They were even hunted by the rats, wicked, unnatural vermin that watched from the shadows. Just their gazes seemed to leech his spirit from his body. Every day he got weaker and weaker from his empty stomach. Soon they would be nibbling on his fingers and toes. He would have nary the strength to swipe at the foul pests. These creatures surely stole souls for the king of Hades.

Barktown's gutters ran with the cursed waters of such deviltry. Should they both be dragged down into the currents? He wasn't rugged enough to save both of them. A man's choice was made by a broken child. No farewells were said. They separated for foraging one early morning, and Kayson left the small burg headed South toward the sea. He had never witnessed the immeasurable ocean, only the endless night of hunger and despair.

Those hungry demons from Barktown had met up with Kayson in the City of a Thousand Sails. They would find he was not the weak alley waif who had abandoned his sister. A hardened warrior tempered by the cruelty of battle stood on these rough streets. He didn't have time for fear, only vengeance for his murdered friend, vengeance for the broken child that chose his life over his sister's. These unholy vermin were using the ghost of Tayla against him. She would have to get in line with the ghosts of all the others he had slain.

Kayson had a plan to draw the abhorrent creatures out from their shadows. If the unholy vermin wanted souls to collect, he would give them an option they couldn't resist. A drunken stroll through the Tumbledown would lure them from their hidey holes seeking a taste of him. The little thing that looked like his sister would crawl out of the night with them, then Kayson would spring his trap with the aid of Makari. Blades and arrows would bring revenge for Delarus.

Makari would need to be sober if his sword arm was to be any help. Kayson stood up on unsteady legs and pulled Makari up too. Kayson would explain more details to his last friend in the world after they both slept and sobered up from grief, fear, and wine.

*

Kayson could just make out the ruins of the grand statue which was the centerpiece of the marketplace. The base was twice as tall as the mercenary and as wide as three ox carts laid end to end. Only two dainty bronze feet, and one well-turned ankle corroded the color of green remained of the once splendid bronze sculpture. Kayson imagined what it must have looked like; all polished and gleaming in the afternoon sun. Peddlers of every vocation crowded below, hocking their wares to the well-to-do out for an afternoon stroll. Now it all lay in ruin, slowly being swallowed by the encroaching sea. The name Tumbledown suited it perfectly. Every poison in the city filtered through this place and settled like an abscess. He could feel the presence of evil deep inside the marrow of his battered bones.

As he pretended to drink from his wineskin, Kayson seeded handfuls of metal crow's feet from a bag he carried. He coughed or laughed every time he cast them, masking the spikes' jangling on the broken cobbles as they landed behind him. One wicked point of the caltrops was always upright, ready to pierce an unwary foe's ill-placed foot. He and Makari learned this trick from crafty Sargent Greylock.

By the Fates, that man hated Delarus, and for good reasons too. Delarus delighted in tormenting the old stager at every opportunity. The worst was when their old friend had snuck into the Sergeant's tent one night and poured honey in his boots. By morning they had attracted a colony of sawtooth aphids which didn't take kindly to Greylock sticking his gnarled foot into their new living space. He couldn't walk for a week after and made Delarus push him around in a wheelbarrow as punishment. Kayson and Makari had never laughed so hard in their lives. Now Delarus was slain, and it was Sergeant Greylock's sage instruction that would aid in their vengeance. Life was a queer circle.

A gleam from his left, and Kayson reared his head toward his brother Makari's position up above where he signaled with a small mirror. While Kayson was out in the open circling the broken statue spreading caltrops in his wake, his ally had taken his best bow and enough arrows to slay a Kaakaran battalion. If the arrows or Kayson's double swords didn't do the bloody work, Kayson had brought two clay containers of powdered drang breath tied together and draped around his neck. A crack of the pots and just a whiff of the sea-infused air would ignite the powder inside, burning the air clear to the harbor. It was his last option, but they would have justice for their murdered friend.

A pale green mist had slowly grown thicker as the night had grown longer. It began to pool thicker around the open marketplace, engulfing him and the statue. Makari's aim would be lost if it grew thicker. Kayson shivered under his alcohol-soaked tunic, doused to cover that his wineskin carried only water. He thought about abandoning tonight's plan and just setting Tumbledown on fire. Burn down the whole damn city and watch the flames grow as their vessel sailed away across Taman Bay.

He heard a caltrop clink and a tiny mewl to his right. Too close. Then a brushing sound and more clinks but no more mewls. They were sweeping his traps away. Smart little demons. The mist had grown higher, almost to his chin. He waved at Makari on high but bade him hold his arrows with a sign. Let them grow closer. Kayson climbed up onto the base of the statue. If he knew the name of the god the statue had been carved for, he would have prayed to it for strength and salvation. Delarus would have spit in its eye. *Clink, clink.*

Piss on the signal. "Fire away, brother! Kill the little bastards!"

Makari fired successive arrows into the area in front of Kayson. Some bit cobblestone, but a few found fleshy purchase; Kayson could tell by the unholy shrieks that followed. He still couldn't see them, but he knew more than a few had been laid down by the hail of Makari's arrows. He shouted, pulled his double shortswords, and made to charge into the green mist, but fear held him fast. What would he find inside the jade haze? Revenge for his dead friend or the doorway to join Delarus and his sister Tayla in Hades?

Makari's shriek drove away those thoughts. He looked up toward his last ally in the world and saw him fall off the edge of the building, an arrow protruding from his back. Oddly, Kayson focused on fletching of the arrow stabbed in his friend's back. Makari took such pride in those colored feathers. A hard thunk reverberated as he bounced on the cobblestone. His groans weren't that far away, and Kayson rushed down off the pedestal to offer aid. He got far enough that the mist was chest-deep before he heard his friend scream in agony. He had witnessed pain in all forms, had born much torment himself, but this wail cut into every fiber of his battle-hardened muscles, not allowing his legs to travel any farther.

"Makari!"

Kayson wobbled back out of the mist onto the base of the broken statue of the nameless god. Even the harvest moon was so frightened it hid behind the clouds. The skittering of little footsteps spread in the mist. He sought to retreat from the rear but heard more skittering behind him. The little demons had flanked him. What creatures strategized like men? He put his back to the sculpted god's good leg, holding his swords at the ready to take a few of the bastards with him.

"Come on! I have teeth and claws too." His voice cracked.

Dying at the foot of a statue wasn't on his agenda. They were supposed to die in battle, not dragged down to become carrion for god-less vermin. They were warriors. He whipped his swords in a menacing pattern to warn away the advancing skittering. He could finally make out a shadowy diminutive form, possibly the waif they encountered the other evening, corrupted by these soulless vermin. His attire bound scraps of discarded rags wrapped around his body even around his head, concealing his features. Except for those blasphemous eyes. Eyes with an iridescent purple sheen. Shimmering unholy eyes that watched his swords tremble in his grip. The urchin stepped toward him away from the swarm of rats.

It began to unwrap its head scarf revealing a visage that could not be possible. His sister Tayla stood in front of him. It had been untold moons and cycles of the sun, but here she stood, looking the same age when he abandoned her. The eyes were the only difference. They were ancient. Rats stood behind her sniffing the air, their tongues flicked tasting his guilt. Eyes were the same purple hue as his sister's.

When he blinked, Tayla was gone. The young boy was standing before him instead. She was never really there. Kayson had left her all the way behind in that Barktown gutter ages ago, but his guilt never left him. It had been packed down deep in his soul through constant battle alongside his blood brothers. This child's face brought all his pain back. He couldn't save his sister, but he wouldn't leave this new child to be corrupted any further. Not this time. This time he wasn't a scared little boy. He was battle-tested and scarred.

Kayson dropped his swords and held one hand out to the urchin with his other hand he grabbed one clay pot possessing the drang's breath. "I surrender, little one. Take my hand and lead me to my fate."

The urchin's face screwed up, confused, but he reached out for the warrior's hand. No sooner had they touched palms did Kayson pull the boy to him and swung him off his feet. The rats swarmed from the mist with ungodly shrieks, seeking the child. Kayson pulled out his clay pots of fiery drang breath, swung them around his head, and slid them across the stones into the mass of vermin. Hoisting the boy over his shoulder, he danced across the courtyard onto the broken statue, climbing as high as he could go.

It was enough to save them both from the blazing explosion that incinerated the mist below. The scorching heat singed his boots enough that he could feel it on his feet. The urchin twisted in his embrace, seeking to join his dying swarm. Their little squeals of anguish didn't penetrate Kayson's heart. Their brethren killed his sworn brothers and had probably corrupted his sister Tayla as well. The urchin cried out in his arms at having lost his family. He didn't know that they were evil, only that he was now alone. Kayson would change that. He would not let this child suffer his sister's fate. Not again.

Kayson held the urchin's cheeks in his hand and made the boy look him in the eye. "My name is Kayson and we are brothers now."

THE LAST EMISSARY

BY: JACK FINN

*T*he elders still tell how Thoron IV, High King of Balaur, died unexpectedly thirty-two years into his reign, passing the Ring of Kings on to his son, Prince Valda. On the morning of his ascension to the throne, Valda fell slain in an ambush set by the king's border lord, Duke Ulgar. Within days, Ulgar launched a series of attacks that eliminated the surviving members of the royal family and declared himself High King. Rebel nobles desperate to foil Ulgar's usurpation enlisted Brosus, a distant cousin of the king, and convinced him to reluctantly accept the Ring of Kings and rally the people of Balaur against Ulgar.

Although a simple man with no aspirations of power, Brosus accepted the ring and the mantle of the true king of Balaur for the good of the people.

For three years, Brosus and his allies fought Ulgar to a bitter stalemate with little hope of either side gaining victory. Then Ulgar, desperate for victory at all costs, formed an unholy alliance with bone mages from the desolate Northlands.

The bone mages, practitioners of the dark arts, could remove a body part from a person or animal and put it on another. Their binding magic enabled the body part to retain all its attributes and functionality, enhancing the recipient.

During the siege of King Brosus' western stronghold at Grantham, survivors claimed units of Duke Ulgar's men possessed legs taken from horses that enabled them to run and kick like beasts. Others of his men had their arms replaced with those of bears with sharp claws and tremendous strength. Survivors of the battle described all manner of amalgamations of man and beast. Even the duke's son, Prince Althair, had a bone mage replace his arm with the arm of a legendary swordsman captured from the Southern Reaches and rode into battle with the limb possessing all the speed and skill of its former owner.

In battle after battle, the king's forces were no match for Ulgar's horde and suffered grievous defeats at Grantham and Folgers Field. With the people suffering under Ulgar's onslaught, King Brosus sent emissaries to Duke Ulgar, seeking to end the war for the kingdom's good. None of the emissaries returned.

In a last desperate attempt to save the kingdom from utter ruin, King Brosus sends the former steward of Grantham, Lord Korlis, as an emissary to Duke Ulgar's court.

Fires burned atop the battlements of Duke Ulgar's castle as the wooden cart guided by Lord Korlis wound its way up the long dirt road. A golden eagle, the sigil of the High King, sewn into the front of his black tunic was the only color on his dark attire as he cast his pale blue eyes up towards the imposing stone fortress.

Peasants lined the roadside dressed in tattered clothes and rags. Their hands outstretched, begging for some coin or a morsel of food. He glanced sidelong at them, noticing their monstrous disfigurements—missing limbs, eyes, and if the rumors true, more intimate body parts. Ulgar's bone mages had harvested their most skilled, attractive, or desirable parts and affixed them to his loyal followers.

A young girl stood among them, her face marred by a gaping hole where a perfect nose once sat. The desperation in her red-rimmed eyes and forlorn gaze forced him to steel his nerves and urge the horse onward toward the fortress.

Armor-clad figures bearing shields and spears lined the imposing stone wall of the fortress as the cart neared the heavy wooden gates. Two guards approached, their spear tips dipping toward Korlis. Heavy plate mail armor, scarred from battle, covered their burly, bearded frames. One man's forehead sprouted two large thick ram horns, the right horn bearing a notch that Korlis imagined came from crushing a battlefield opponent's helmeted skull.

"I am Lord Korlis, emissary of King Brosus. I am unarmed and bear a message for Duke Ulgar."

Korlis swept his black cape wide, to reveal his empty sword belt.

"Another emissary for King Ulgar," the one with the horns snorted, and both guards laughed maliciously. "I am sure he will be pleased to have some entertainment for the evening."

"What is this?" He peered back into the bed of the cart at the shroud-wrapped bundle.

"A peace offering for Duke Ulgar."

"*King* Ulgar!" sneered horns.

"It is a gift from my lord to yours." Korlis was unmoved by the guards' threatening tone and posture.

"Open the gates!" The horned guard yelled out to those atop the wall, and Korlis heard the command repeated inside the courtyard within.

The two thick wooden gates slowly opened inward to reveal a torchlit courtyard lined with heavily armed soldiers. The horned guard gestured for Korlis to ease the cart forward slowly, and he complied. Warily, the two guards marched beside the cart, spears at ready.

Korlis passed through the darkened entryway and out into the light of the courtyard. He glanced sidelong at the men that lined the yard; all bore curved boar tusks protruding from their lower jaw, an addition from the bone mages that identified them as Ulgar's personal guard. The light of the torches cast ominous elongated shadows of the armored men along the inner walls of the fortress.

The horned guard gestured for him to stop the cart, and Korlis reined the horse to a halt. A boar-tusked guard stepped out from the line of men and grabbed the reins from his hand. He grabbed Korlis by the arm with his other hand and pulled him down from the cart.

Ulgar's men snickered as Korlis tumbled down from the cart and lost his footing; he barely regained his balance to prevent sprawling in the dusty courtyard. The tusked guard pushed him up against the wooden side of the cart and roughly ran his hands along Korlis' body, searching for weapons. Satisfied Korlis was unarmed, the guard shoved him against the cart again and expelled a mouthful of rancid breath into his face.

"No weapons." The tusked guard nodded to the horned guard.

The horned guard grabbed Korlis by the arm and led him roughly across the courtyard. Sneering men with hateful eyes parted to let them pass. Two tusked guards opened a pair of wooden doors the height of two men and allowed them entry into the throne room.

Korlis felt all eyes in the room turn towards them as they entered. His eyes cast about as the horned guard ushered him forward. At the front of the room, a half dozen stone braziers blazed, illuminating three stone-hewn thrones. On the center and largest thrown sat Ulgar, draped in furs and staring intently at Korlis with a dark, brooding gaze. He stroked his long black beard thoughtfully as the horned guard pushed the emissary down the hall toward the thrones.

Behind Ulgar stood his wife, Lady Corrinne, a tall blonde woman with unremarkable features except for the intense, cunning glare of her light green eyes. She rested a long-fingered hand on Ulgar's shoulder as if she was keeping a dog at bay.

Beside Ulgar sat a young blonde boy on a smaller throne; Korlis knew this must be Ulgar's youngest son, Lord Blaine. The boy sat with a monstrously obese white rabbit in his lap, and his pale hand stroked it lovingly. The throne to Ulgar's right sat empty.

Korlis cast his eyes about the room and noted that Ulgar's court was a mix of the beautiful and the bizarre. Many of the ladies of the court boasted perfect noses, eyes of two different colors, or ample breasts that Korlis suspected were appropriated from peasants unfortunate enough to have desirable features for the nobility. Other ladies had features taken from animals. Korlis noticed with incredulity that many women had replaced their noses with tiny, delicate birdlike beaks or the whiskered noses of some unfortunate feline.

Standing together were Ulgar's war chiefs, all bearded and tusked like the guards. They cast smug looks at Korlis, sneering at the emissary of a nearly defeated foe. Other warriors meandered about the hall, some with the legs of horses or clawed arms of bears. Several other warriors had the long muzzle and sharp teeth of wolves. All wore armor and carried long curved swords at their waist.

Above him, all was darkness, but Korlis had little doubt that archers sat poised on the balconies above, ready to rain deadly arrows on any threat. He knew too well how accurate their enhanced eyesight could be even in near total darkness. Under the pitch black night of a new moon, Ulgar's archers decimated the men standing the battlements of Korlis' castle. The memory of that terror-filled night came rushing back to Korlis, knotting his stomach. The whoosh of arrows rising from darkness. The tell-tale crunch of shafts punching through armor. The startled cry of stricken soldiers and thud of their body upon the stone walkways. The frustrated curses of his own archers as their human eyes failed to find targets for their wrath in the coal-black night.

"King Ulgar." Lady Corrine's voice was high-pitched and grating. "This man wears the symbol of the false king. It offends me."

The horned guard grabbed Korlis by the collar, stopping his progression toward the thrones. A soldier with the thick dark-furred arms of a bear stepped in front of the emissary and looked to-ward Ulgar. The king silently nodded his head at the soldier.

A fiendish smile of glee crossed the soldier's face as he turned to Korlis. He suppressed the urge to retreat from the man, refusing to give the soldier the satisfaction of showing fear. The horned guard held him fast at the collar as the soldier swiped his clawed hands across Korlis' chest in powerful strokes. The man's claws tore through fabric and skin as he ripped free the front of Korlis' tunic bearing the golden eagle emblem of Brosus. Thick rivulets of blood ran down Korlis' chest from the deep scratches criss-crossing his torso. The rending of his flesh be-neath the man's claws assailed his mind with a sudden wave of pain. Korlis was no stranger to injury, he was a professional soldier and his body bore the scars of a dozen more grievous wounds. Steeling himself against the pain, he ex-haled slowly letting the sensation dissipate and refusing to give them the satisfaction of crying out. The soldier dropped the tattered fabric with the golden eagle emblem to the floor and spat on it to the uproarious cheers and jeers of the court.

"The emissary smells of eucalyptus." The soldier made an exaggerated gesture of sniffing Korlis before turning to the assembled court and throwing his arms wide. "And fear!" The members of the court laughed heartily at the soldier's words.

The horned guard pushed Korlis toward the thrones, and the emissary caught sight of black-hooded figures in the dark corner of the room: the bone mages.

"Kneel before the king." The horned guard struck the back of Korlis' knees with his spear shaft, dropping the emissary to his knees.

Korlis grimaced as his knees struck the hard stone floor, but he kept his gaze on Ulgar's bearded face. He had mentally prepared himself for such treatment. The emissaries sent before him gave their lives in service to the High King, and undeniably suffered horrifically at the hands of these dishonorable men. The cruelty of Ulgar's court seemed to know no bounds, and that prospect terrified Korlis. He knew these wicked men would revel at inflicting a degree of suffering that could make a man beg to all that was holy for the sweet respite of death. Korlis was most deeply troubled by how the bone-mages could wield their dark powers to that end. However, he would not let his fears distract him from his mission. An emissary was the physical embodiment of their sovereign, and it was long the custom of the land to treat them as such. In turn, emissaries expected to conduct themselves with the dignity of the office bestowed upon them. These men debased themselves by their behavior, Korlis would not.

"I am an emissary of Brosus, High King of Balaur," Korlis' voice belied none of the fear that was roiling in his guts.

The room erupted with angry shouts. The horned guard stepped before the kneeling emissary and bent to hold his face close to Korlis'. Malice filled the guard's beady eyes as he reared his head back and butted Korlis with his curling ram's horns.

The angry shouts of the room turned to roaring laughter and cheers as Korlis' head snapped back, and a bloody gash opened on his forehead that sent streaks of blood running down his face and into his eyes.

The blow to the head caused Korlis to reel for a moment before regaining his balance as he tried to blink the blood from his eyes. The laughter in the room stopped abruptly as Ulgar raised his hand for silence.

"An emissary from Brosus," Ulgar mused. "Where did we put those other emissaries from dear Brosus?"

"Right here, my lord." A man dressed in a bright green tunic with tasseled bells haphazardly hanging from it stepped from the crowd. The man had long rabbit ears and the tail of a cow; in his hand, he carried a long stick with four desiccated heads affixed to the shaft by chains that ran through their ears. "The emissaries are right here!

The man's attire jingled as he shook the stick to make the heads bob. Korlis knew these brave men, and he shuddered at what they must have experienced before their death and desecration.

Ulgar laughed deeply at the sight, and the room joined in with hoots and cackles of delight.

"I know this man." A melodic voice rang above the laughter. "You are Lord Korlis, Steward of Grantham."

"*Former* Steward of Grantham," one of the war chiefs called out to a new chorus of laughter.

Korlis looked sidelong at the man who stepped from the crowd. He was a tall blonde man with immaculately clean armor that reflected the firelight. His skin was pale white except for his right arm, which was jet black like the men of the Southern Reaches.

"Lord Althair." Korlis nodded respectfully, showing the proper deference an emissary to the son of duke, and tried to blink some of the blood from his eyes.

"Oh yes, I remember now." Althair circled Korlis menacingly and addressed the court. "You fought alongside Brosus . . . and lost. Your family, a wife, and daughter, I believe, fled with your household staff into the swamps of Shylee.

"Now, whatever became of them? Oh yes, I recall now. They were set upon by craze hornets in the swamp. Oh, such terrible things, craze hornets. One sting from them and poof." The man snapped his finger in front of Korlis' face. "You become like a crazed beast and tear each other apart. Lord Korlis." Althair lowered his face close to Korlis. "Do you ever wonder if it was your wife who tore your daughter to shreds or your daughter who tore the flesh from your beloved?"

Korlis' face remained impassive, but inside, he seethed with rage and fought the desire to grab Althair and tear out his throat before the horned guard could run him through with his spear. No, he was King Brosus' emissary, the kingdom's last chance for peace. He would not let this upstart pretender prince provoke him. He would not fail in his mission.

"Father." Blaine stopped petting his rabbit for a moment and put his hand on his father's arm. "Father, the man has such beautiful eyes. I would like one for my rabbit."

Korlis felt a pit of horror turn in his stomach as Ulgar turned and looked at him appraisingly. A smile of pure malice crossed Ulgar's face, and he patted his young son on the leg as he beckoned one of the dark-robed bone mages forward.

The horned guard gripped Korlis' collar and grabbed a handful of the emissary's hair, yanking his face upward. Korlis tried to wrestle free, but two tusked guards grabbed his arms and held him tight.

The dark-robed mage seemed to glide towards him, a thin bony hand reaching for Korlis' face. Korlis could see the pale, wizened face of the mage deep within the confines of the hood. The face was expressionless, and the man's piercing gray eyes clouded with intense concentration.

Korlis tried to screw his eyes shut as the bony hand covered his right eye; the mage's skin was ice cold and chilled him to his core. A searing pain burst from his eye into the back of his skull, and Korlis could not stymie the scream emanating from his lips. His body trembled as he fought against the lightning strikes of pain that continued to flash inside his head to regain his composure.

Darkness replaced the vision in his right eye, and he wavered from the pain and disorientation that came with his loss of depth perception. Through the pain and the blood, his one remaining eye watched the mage place a hand over the obese rabbit's eye. The creature squealed uncomfortably for a moment, but when the mage stepped back, Korlis' pale blue eye peered forth from the creature's head.

"Oh, Father, isn't it wonderful." Blaine lifted the rabbit and stared gleefully into its face.

"King Brosus is dead." Korlis forced the words out through gritted teeth as his eye socket throbbed.

"What's that?" Althair leaned closer as all attention turned towards the emissary.

"King Brosus is dead; Queen Amaron has sent me with an offer of peace," Korlis said loud enough for all in the hall to hear.

"What trickery is this?" Ulgar leaned forward and peered intently at the emissary.

"He lies, Father." Althair drew his sword with his dark-skinned hand. "Let me take his head."

"It is no lie." Korlis stared into Ulgar's face with his one good eye. "I have brought with me King Brosus' body. It is in the wooden cart outside.

Queen Amaron wishes only peace between our peoples."

"Bring me this body." Ulgar bellowed the order, and two tusked guards quickly exited the hall.

All eyes turned towards the tall wooden doors when they reopened, and the guards hurriedly carried the shrouded body into the hall. Murmurs ran through the crowd as the shrouded body was brought before Ulgar and unceremoniously dropped. Korlis winced as the body thudded against the stone floor.

Ulgar gestured toward the body, and the two guards cut the ropes that bound it and yanked off the gray shroud. A gasp rose among those assembled, and even Ulgar showed unmitigated shock as he stared down at the lifeless body of Brosus, one-time High King of Balaur.

Korlis looked sadly at the body of his sovereign, his handsome face so peaceful in death, a peace that had escaped him during the entirety of his short reign. The emissary saw Ulgar lean forward, and the man's eyes opened wide in shock as he spied the Ring of Kings still on Brosus' finger.

"Bring me the ring," Ulgar hissed with desire. Althair moved forward to remove the ring, but Ulgar held up a hand, stopping him, and gestured to the bone mage. "No, bring me the whole finger."

The bone mage bowed his hooded head in acquiescence and stepped towards the body.

"Father, that man is still alive." Blaine leaned forward and peered at the body.

A hush filled the room as all eyes looked intently at the still form of Brosus. Korlis stared as well and could detect the most subtle signs of the king's chest rising and falling.

"My lord, the prince is right; this man is breathing." The bone mage's voice was a shallow rasping sound.

Korlis squinted his remaining eye and saw the king's chest almost pulsing more than rising and falling. He allowed only the slightest hint of a tight smile to cross lips.

"Well, he will most certainly be dead now." Althair raised his curved sword and cleaved it down onto the king's chest.

Rather than slice down into living flesh, Althair's sword collapsed the king's chest as if he struck a hollow melon.

"What sort of trickery is this?" Ulgar gasped.

From within the hollow of the king's chest burst forth thousands of black, red-winged insects: craze hornets. The creatures buzzed angrily as they swarmed upon the bone mage and Althair, stinging them as their screams echoed through the hall.

"You did this." The horned guard ran the point of his blade through Korlis' chest only moments before the winged creatures unleashed their primal wrath upon him as well.

Korlis dropped to the floor, his lifeblood pouring out of his body like a deep red river. He saw Althair, crazed from the hornet stings, decapitate the bone mage before the horned guard leaped upon him and head-butted the pretender prince repeatedly until both their skulls split wide open. Ulgar's court turned upon itself as the stings of the craze hornets spread their madness. Men and women bit and tore at each other, rending each other until their flesh hung in crimson shreds.

Ulgar and Corinne, covered in hornet stings, rolled on the ground in a maddened tangle, ripping chunks of flesh from each other. The obese rabbit, maddened with stings, tore out Blaine's throat with its teeth and claws. In the corner, the bone mages rolled on the floor, slashing and scratching at each other.

The room had descended into complete chaos as Ulgar's people rendered each other into shredded corpses. Hearing the screams, the guards in the outer courtyard rushed inside, freeing the hornets and spreading their madness to the soldiers outside.

In the distance, Korlis heard the war horns of Queen Amaron's army, swathed in eucalyptus balm to protect them from the hornets, as they advanced on Ulgar's doomed fortress.

Korlis lay alongside his friend and king, pleased that Queen Amaron would find them side by side at the end. As his vision began to fade, Korlis stared at the serene, bearded face of King Brosus and recalled their last conversation.

"Korlis, I know you have grieved your family's loss, as have I. Your daughter was like a granddaughter to me. I see how you charge recklessly in battle, seeking death to join your wife and daughter in the afterlife. The mission you have volunteered for will grant you that death, but it will also avenge the murder of our families, and most importantly, it will save the kingdom.

The fine wine I sip contains the extract of a poison berry; my death will be swift but painless. Once I have crossed over from this world, my body will be specially prepared as a vessel containing six craze hornet nests the royal beekeepers have carefully cultivated. If I know Ulgar, he will not hesitate to defile my body, and by doing so, he will unleash his death within. You must succeed in getting my body into Ulgar's hall at all costs. This is your mission. You must not fail. You are my most trusted friend. You are my last emissary."

THE BLACK ALTAR

BY: JP WILDER

Rothar adjusted the battered leather strap of his sword belt, grimacing as he scanned the dimly lit tavern. It had been a rare moment of calm for him and Leena, fresh off a hard-fought victory, and for once, HollowGate seemed content to let them be. The air inside the tavern was thick with the scent of smoke and ale, a buzz of conversation filling the corners as townsfolk swapped stories over clinking mugs. Rothar was just lifting his drink when the door crashed open, and a figure lurched in, staggering under the weight of something unseen.

The man's hood slipped back, revealing a pale, dirt-streaked face, his eyes wild and unfocused. His breath came in gasps, his hands clutching something tightly to his chest. Blood trickled from his mouth, leaving dark trails down his chin as he stumbled forward, collapsing in a heap at Rothar's feet. A murmur rippled through the tavern, patrons recoiling, eyes wide as whispers swept through the crowd.

"The Black Altar . . ." the man gasped, each word strained, his voice a raspy whisper. He clutched at Rothar's boot, fingers cold and trembling as he lifted a small, gleaming object—a black, jagged amulet that caught the light like a drop of ink suspended in glass.

Rothar leaned down, the hair on his arms prickling. He knew better than to touch relics like these—objects that seemed to drink in the light, pulsing with a power that was dark, oily, and cold. He glanced at Leena, whose gaze was locked on the amulet, her expression grim.

"It's . . . coming for me," the man wheezed, eyes darting around the room as if he could already see whatever terror was pursuing him. "For all of us." With a final, desperate look, he pressed the amulet into Rothar's hand, his fingers dropping limply before his eyes rolled back and his body slumped to the floor, lifeless.

The tavern went still, a silence falling so thick Rothar could hear his own heartbeat pounding in his ears. He could feel the weight of the amulet pressing into his palm, colder than ice. Around them, murmurs started to rise, fear creeping into the voices of the patrons who began backing away, whispering hurried prayers under their breath.

Rothar stared at the amulet, feeling a heaviness settle over him. Leena's eyes met his, her face pale and tense.

"You feel it?" she whispered, barely audible, her voice laced with unease.

Rothar nodded, glancing at the lifeless man sprawled at their feet. "Whatever this thing is . . . it's cursed."

The door opened again, but this time it wasn't a lone, desperate figure. A group of cloaked figures, their faces hidden behind dark hoods, slipped into the tavern one by one. The crowd went silent, watching as the newcomers fanned out, blocking the exits with practiced precision. They moved with a purpose, their eyes locked onto Rothar and Leena, flicking briefly to the amulet glinting in Rothar's hand.

The leader stepped forward, his voice cold and commanding. "The amulet is ours," he said, his hand extended. "Return it, and perhaps we'll let you live."

Rothar scoffed, gripping the amulet tightly as he slipped it into his belt pouch. He'd dealt with HollowGate's dark circles before, but the calm, calculating menace radiating from this group was unsettling, like a predator toying with its prey.

"You're welcome to try and take it," he replied, his voice low and dangerous. Beside him, Leena's fingers twitched, readying a spell, her gaze never leaving the leader.

The cloaked man gave a tight smile. "Have it your way."

Without warning, the cultists surged forward, blades flashing as they moved with deadly precision. Rothar barely had time to draw his sword before they were upon him, and the tavern erupted into chaos. He swung his blade, the metallic ring of steel meeting steel echoing in the small space. Leena was beside him, her hand flaring with blue light as she cast a blast of energy that sent two cultists crashing backward.

A patron screamed, diving under a table as another cultist leapt forward, dagger aimed at Rothar's heart. He twisted, the blade grazing his side as he slammed his elbow into the man's jaw, sending him sprawling to the floor. Around them, tables overturned, tankards of ale splashed across the wooden planks, and the smell of smoke filled the air as someone knocked over a lantern in the fray.

Rothar parried another strike, his muscles coiling with each blow as he fought off the attackers. "Leena, we've got to get out of here," he shouted, eyes darting to the windows where more hooded figures gathered, watching with predatory patience.

Leena's gaze was steely as she dispatched another cultist with a quick, brutal spell, her charm glowing fiercely against her chest. "Agreed," she said, grabbing a nearby mug and hurling it at a cultist's head with surprising accuracy.

They fought their way to the nearest window, Leena casting a blast that shattered the glass in an explosion of sound and glittering shards. Rothar ducked through, feeling the sting of broken glass as he landed heavily on the cobblestone outside. Leena followed, her feet barely touching the ground as she spun around, firing another blast to cover their escape.

The street was empty, eerie in the pre-dawn quiet, the only sound their heavy breathing as they sprinted down an alley, twisting and turning through HollowGate's maze of narrow streets. Rothar's heart thundered in his chest, the amulet a cold weight at his side. Behind them, he could hear the cultists' footsteps, their pursuit relentless.

They ducked into a hidden passageway, pressing themselves against the damp stone walls. Rothar caught his breath, glancing at Leena. Her eyes were sharp, calculating, and there was a glint there that told him she was already piecing together the threat they were facing.

"The Black Altar . . ." she whispered, voice tight. "I've heard tales of a cult that worshiped it—a power that was supposed to have been destroyed ages ago. . . in the Soul Wars—the First Ruin."

"Clearly, they're back," Rothar replied, jaw clenched, swallowing a lump. Nothing that hearkened from the time before the First Ruin could prove to be anything but corrupt. The amulet pulsed at his side, a reminder of the curse they now carried. "And I doubt they'll stop until they get this."

The footsteps grew louder, the cultists closing in. Rothar met Leena's gaze, a silent promise passing between them. They'd survived worse, but something told him this was only the beginning.

Rothar barely had time to catch his breath before the cultists' footsteps drew closer, echoing through the labyrinthine alleys. He glanced at Leena, who was already reaching for the charm at her neck, her fingers tightening around it as she muttered a quick incantation. Her face was set in grim determination, blue eyes blazing with defiance against the shadows pooling around them.

"This way," Leena whispered, grabbing Rothar's arm and pulling him into another alleyway, narrower and darker than the last. The damp stone walls loomed close, dripping with moisture and shrouded in the faint stench of decay. Rothar's hand instinctively went to the hilt of his sword as they pushed forward, each step muffled by the slick, uneven cobblestones beneath their feet.

They rounded a corner, only to stop dead as three cloaked figures blocked their path. The cultists were silent, faces hidden in shadow, their weapons glinting under the faint light of a hanging lantern. The alley was a narrow choke point, with no room to maneuver or retreat. Rothar felt his pulse quicken, adrenaline surging as he calculated their odds.

"Give us the amulet," one of the cultists hissed, his voice cold and sibilant, like steel sliding over ice. He held a thin, curved blade that shimmered with an unnatural sheen, the metal seeming to drink in the darkness around it.

"Sorry," Rothar replied, his tone mocking as he drew his sword. "We've grown attached."

The cultist's eyes narrowed beneath his hood, and with a sharp command in a language Rothar didn't recognize, the three surged forward, blades flashing. Rothar met the first cultist head-on, his sword clashing against the man's dagger in a burst of sparks. The force of the impact reverberated up Rothar's arm, but he held firm, twisting to drive his shoulder into the cultist's chest and forcing him back.

The second cultist lunged at Leena, her dagger flashing toward Leena's throat. Leena ducked, rolling away from the blade as she chanted an incantation, her charm flaring with blue light. A gust of energy erupted from her hand, hitting the cultist square in the chest and sending him crashing into the wall, stunned.

Rothar sidestepped another strike, narrowly avoiding the sharp edge of the third cultist's blade. He retaliated with a swift slash, the blade catching the cultist across the arm. The man staggered back, his grip faltering just long enough for Rothar to deliver a final, brutal strike.

The cultist dropped to the ground, his weapon clattering against the cobblestones.

Leena was already back on her feet, magic crackling in her hand as she turned to face the remaining cultist. The man hesitated, eyes flicking between Leena's glowing charm and Rothar's blood-streaked sword. He took a step back, then another, before retreating into the shadows with a hiss of frustration.

Rothar exhaled, glancing at Leena. "We can't keep doing this. They'll wear us down."

Leena's eyes were dark, her expression set with a fierce resolve. "We have to keep moving. The longer we hold onto this amulet, the more of them will come. But we can't let them have it—not after what we've seen."

Rothar nodded, slipping the amulet from his pouch and studying it under the faint light of the alley. The obsidian surface was smooth, cold, and unsettling, like holding a piece of night itself. It felt wrong in his hand, as if it were a living thing that pulsed with a dark energy.

"This thing is dangerous," Rothar muttered, almost to himself. "But there's got to be more to it than just an amulet."

"More than you know," a voice rasped from above.

Rothar and Leena froze, both turning as a shadowy figure dropped down from the rooftop above them, landing with barely a sound. It was Draven—an ex-mercenary Rothar had fought alongside in his past life, before HollowGate had claimed them both. Draven's expression was hidden beneath his hood, but Rothar could feel his gaze, sharp and assessing.

"Draven," Rothar said, voice tense. "Didn't expect to see you with this lot."

Draven's mouth twisted into a humorless smile. "You left me no choice when you took that amulet. I'm here to get it back. Hand it over, and I'll make sure they don't skin you alive."

Rothar tightened his grip on his sword. "Not happening."

Draven tilted his head, almost amused. "You don't know what you're dealing with, Rothar. The Black Altar is more than a cult. They're looking to open something—a gateway. The amulet is the key. You hand it over, or they'll tear HollowGate apart to get it."

Leena stepped forward, her gaze cold. "And you're just their pawn?"

Draven shrugged, a gleam of something dangerous in his eyes. "Survival, Leena. You remember what that's like, don't you? Or have you become too noble for it?"

Rothar took a step forward, placing himself between Draven and Leena. "So, that's it, then? You're just going to sell your soul for a chance to live a little longer?"

Draven's expression hardened. "Better than dying for something that doesn't matter. But if you want to play the hero, I'm not about to stand in your way."

Before Rothar could respond, Draven lunged, his blade arcing toward Rothar's chest. Rothar parried, gritting his teeth as he blocked the next strike, each blow delivered with the ruthless precision of a seasoned fighter. Draven was stronger than the cultists, faster, and he fought with a deadly focus that sent a thrill of danger through Rothar's veins.

The clash of their swords echoed through the narrow alley, sparks flying with each collision. Rothar deflected a vicious jab, twisting to deliver a counter-strike that glanced off Draven's shoulder. Draven grunted, his expression twisting with frustration as he pressed forward, his blade slashing in a quick, relentless flurry.

Leena moved to intervene, but Draven twisted, ducking under Rothar's guard and knocking Leena's feet out from under her with a swift kick. She hit the ground hard, gasping as Draven turned back to Rothar, his blade glinting as he advanced.

"You don't have to do this," Rothar said, his voice low, his eyes locked on Draven's. "We've fought together before. There's still time to turn back."

Draven's expression softened for a split second, the barest flicker of hesitation in his eyes. But it was gone as quickly as it had come, replaced by a cold resolve that left no room for doubt.

"Not this time, Rothar," he replied, voice laced with finality.

Rothar swung his blade in a last, desperate strike, his muscles straining as he forced Draven back. They were evenly matched, each attack countered with brutal efficiency, neither willing to give an inch. But Rothar could feel his strength waning, his grip slipping as the weight of the fight began to wear on him.

Leena's voice cut through the chaos, her chant rising in intensity as she raised her charm, casting a burst of light that flared like a miniature sun. Draven staggered, momentarily blinded, and Rothar took the opening, driving his shoulder into Draven's chest and slamming him against the wall. Draven struggled, cursing, but Rothar's grip was unyielding.

"This is your last chance," Rothar said, breathing hard. "Walk away."

Draven's eyes burned with defiance, but he said nothing, his body going limp as Rothar held him there, the weight of their shared past heavy in the silence. At last, he wrenched free, slipping back into the shadows with a final, bitter look.

As his footsteps faded, Rothar turned to Leena, who was already gathering her strength, her face pale but determined.

"We have to keep moving," she said, her voice steady despite the tremor in her hands. "Draven's right about one thing—the Black Altar is more than just a cult. They're planning something big, and the amulet is the key. If we don't get to the Black Altar before they do . . ."

"But where is this—"

"I know, Rothar. I know things since . . ."

Rothar nodded, he knew what she was about to say, and he'd rather not know the things his companion knew. Whether it was sorcery or her knowledge of the dark histories of this land, magic—and its corruption—came easy to Leena. "Never mind," he said, slipping the amulet back into his pouch. "We'll have a lot more to worry about than just Draven."

They exchanged a look, a silent understanding passing between them as they turned and slipped into the shadows, ready to face whatever horrors awaited them beneath the streets of HollowGate.

They moved swiftly through HollowGate's winding alleys, the morning mist settling over the city like a shroud. Every corner held shadows that seemed darker than usual, every sound was amplified by the echoing silence of the city holding its breath. Rothar felt the weight of the amulet in his pouch, like a dark pulse that synced with his heartbeat, a reminder of the power it carried—and the danger it invited.

Leena walked beside him, her face tight with focus, her hand grazing the charm at her neck as she muttered protective spells. Rothar knew she could feel it too—the strange energy that radiated from the amulet, as if it were alive, hungry.

"We're close," she whispered, nodding toward a broken archway that marked the entrance to an underground passage. "The Black Altar's sanctuary is beneath the city, where the old sewers and catacombs converge."

Rothar grunted, glancing around. "Let's get this done. The faster we rid ourselves of this thing, the better."

They ducked through the archway and descended into the darkness below. The air grew colder, damp with the scent of stagnant water and mildew. Rothar's eyes adjusted to the dimness, his grip on his sword tightening as they moved deeper. The amulet seemed to throb, its power resonating with something unseen, something vast.

Leena paused, fingers brushing the damp stone walls. Strange symbols were carved into the stone, barely visible in the faint light. They twisted and looped, forming shapes that seemed to shift when he tried to focus on them.

"These marks . . ." she murmured, trailing her hand over one of the carvings. "They're ancient. Older than HollowGate itself. This place was built for something dark, Rothar. Something forgotten."

"Then let's make sure it stays that way," he replied, casting a wary glance down the passage. The faintest hint of a chant drifted up from the darkness below, a low, rhythmic murmur that settled into his bones like an ache. Rothar's jaw tightened. The cult was close.

They crept forward, each step echoing softly in the silence. The chanting grew louder, filling the air with a sound that was almost tangible. Rothar could feel it pressing against him, seeping into his skin, curling around his thoughts. Leena's breath came faster, her fingers twitching as the chant grew stronger.

"Whatever they're summoning," she whispered, her eyes wide with dread, "it's powerful."

The passage opened into a cavernous chamber, dimly lit by flickering torches set into the walls. At the center of the room, a raised stone altar loomed, its surface etched with the same twisted symbols that lined the walls. Hooded figures surrounded it, their faces hidden as they chanted, their voices blending into a dark, harmonic murmur that filled the chamber.

Rothar's eyes fixed on the figure standing at the altar, their arms raised high, fingers curled around a dark, ornate dagger. The cult leader's hood was pulled back, revealing a face that was almost skeletal, skin stretched tight over sharp bones, eyes that glinted with an unholy light.

"Tonight," the leader intoned, their voice echoing through the chamber, "we awaken the Whispering One! The darkness shall rise, and we will be its vessels!"

The cultists raised their voices, the chant swelling into a fevered pitch that reverberated off the walls. Rothar's skin prickled, the air thickening with a malevolent energy that seemed to radiate from the altar itself.

Leena grabbed his arm, her voice urgent. "We have to stop them before they complete the ritual."

Rothar nodded, slipping the amulet from his pouch and glancing at it one last time. The obsidian surface was cold, pulsing faintly with a darkness that felt almost sentient. He tightened his grip, feeling a surge of determination.

Together, they stepped into the light, their presence drawing the attention of the cultists. The chanting faltered as hooded heads turned, eyes narrowing in recognition and anger. The leader's gaze fixed on Rothar, a twisted smile spreading across his face.

"You dare to bring the amulet here?" the leader sneered, his voice dripping with scorn. "It belongs to the altar, to the Whispering One. Surrender it, and perhaps I'll grant you a quick death."

"Come take it," Rothar replied, his voice hard as he drew his sword. The blade caught the torchlight, gleaming with the promise of blood. Beside him, Leena's charm flared with a soft, blue light, casting an eerie glow over her face.

The cultists surged forward, their movements swift and precise, weapons glinting as they descended upon them. Rothar swung his sword, meeting the first attacker with a powerful strike that sent the cultist sprawling. Another lunged at him, blade slicing through the air, but he dodged, driving his elbow into the cultist's ribs before bringing his sword down in a deadly arc.

Leena's voice rose in a chant, her fingers weaving patterns in the air as bolts of blue energy shot from her hands, striking the cultists and sending them reeling. Her magic crackled in the air, the blue light illuminating her fierce expression as she held her ground.

A cultist slipped through their defenses, dagger raised as they closed in on Leena's back. Rothar saw the movement, his pulse quickening as he twisted, intercepting the attacker with a brutal strike. The cultist fell, eyes wide with shock as Rothar turned back to the fight, every muscle taut with focus.

The leader watched them from the altar, his smile widening as he raised the dagger high. "Your resistance is futile," he sneered, voice echoing with an unnatural resonance. "The Whispering One will consume you all."

He plunged the dagger into the altar, the blade sinking into the stone as if it were flesh. The room trembled, the ground beneath their feet shifting as a dark, pulsing energy erupted from the altar, filling the chamber with an overwhelming, suffocating power.

Rothar staggered, the force pressing down on him like a weight. He could feel it clawing at his mind, whispering promises of power, visions of darkened lands, cities crumbling under his command. He shook his head, forcing himself to focus, to push past the whispers.

"Leena!" he shouted, his voice strained. "We have to break the connection!"

Leena's face was pale, her eyes distant as she fought against the pull of the altar's power. She raised her hands, fingers trembling as she chanted, her voice steady despite the fear that flickered in her gaze.

With a final, desperate surge of energy, she unleashed a wave of light that slammed into the altar, cracking its surface. The cult leader let out a furious scream, his gaze turning wild as he raised his hands, directing the energy toward her.

The wave of darkness hit Leena with a force that sent her reeling, her body slamming into the stone wall behind her. She collapsed, gasping, her fingers scrabbling for her charm as she tried to regain her focus.

Rothar's vision blurred with rage as he charged forward, cutting down another cultist in his path. He reached the altar, eyes locked on the cult leader, whose expression shifted from fury to fear.

"You won't win," the leader hissed, his voice dripping with venom.

Rothar's response was a low growl as he drove his sword into the leader's chest, the blade sinking deep as the man let out a strangled gasp, his eyes widening with shock. The cult leader crumpled, his body hitting the ground in a lifeless heap.

The energy radiating from the altar wavered, the whispers fading as the power dissipated. Rothar staggered back, chest heaving as he turned to find Leena.

She was struggling to her feet, one hand pressed against the wall for support. Her gaze met his, a flicker of relief passing over her face as she nodded, her voice a hoarse whisper. "It's done. The connection is broken."

Rothar moved to her side, steadying her as they watched the last remnants of the cultists scatter, their morale shattered along with their leader. The room fell silent, the oppressive weight lifting as the power of the altar faded into nothing.

As they turned to leave, Rothar felt the weight of the amulet in his pouch, a reminder of the darkness they had fought against—and the power that still lingered, waiting to be unleashed.

Rothar and Leena moved through the abandoned streets, keeping to the shadows as HollowGate slowly returned to life around them. The storm had broken, and the rain had left a damp, misty chill that clung to the city, blanketing it in an eerie quiet. They made their way toward the edge of town, the weight of the amulet in Rothar's pouch pressing against his side like a heartbeat.

Leena's breathing was shallow, her skin still pale and slick with sweat from the battle. But her eyes were sharp, focused, even though exhaustion tugged at her with every step. The blue light from her charm had dimmed, its energy spent, leaving her vulnerable but resolute.

"We need to get rid of this thing," she muttered, casting a wary glance at the pouch where the amulet was tucked. "As long as it's here, HollowGate isn't safe."

Rothar grunted, nodding in agreement. "Problem is, where? We can't just throw it in the river and hope for the best. This thing . . . it's alive somehow. It'll find its way back."

They reached the outskirts of the city, where the old stone buildings thinned and gave way to rolling hills and thick, dense woods. Rothar paused, glancing back at the shadowed skyline of HollowGate, a frown creasing his brow.

"If we want to destroy it, we're going to need help," he said, his voice quiet but edged with determination. "Someone who knows more about this kind of magic."

Leena's gaze drifted toward the treeline, her expression contemplative. "I know someone," she said after a moment, voice hesitant. "But it's risky. She's . . . unpredictable."

"Unpredictable how?" Rothar asked, his tone wary.

Leena's lips twisted into a wry smile. "She has a habit of taking as much as she gives. And she's not exactly fond of outsiders."

"Better than letting this thing fester," he replied, and together, they turned toward the woods, stepping into the shadowed path that led to the edge of HollowGate's borders.

The forest closed around them, the thick canopy blocking out what little light remained, casting the path into near-total darkness. Rothar's grip tightened on his sword hilt as they moved deeper, every rustle and creak of the branches putting him on edge. The amulet in his pouch seemed to pulse with a dark energy, resonating with something in the forest, as if it sensed an ally nearby.

After what felt like hours, they reached a small clearing where a circle of stones stood, ancient and moss-covered, each one etched with strange symbols that seemed to glow faintly in the dim light. A figure waited in the center, draped in a cloak of deep green that blended seamlessly with the shadows around her.

Leena stepped forward, her voice soft but firm. "Mara. We need your help."

The woman turned, her face half-hidden beneath her hood, eyes gleaming like embers in the darkness. She was older than Leena but radiated a raw, untamed energy that set Rothar on edge.

She looked him up and down, a smirk tugging at the corner of her mouth.

"So, this is your hired sword," she said, her voice rich and mocking. "Does he know what he's carrying?"

Rothar bristled, but Leena placed a calming hand on his arm, nodding toward the woman. "He knows enough," she replied. "We need to destroy it, Mara. Before it destroys Hollow-Gate—and us."

Mara's gaze shifted to Rothar's pouch, her eyes narrowing as she studied it with an intensity that made him uncomfortable. She stepped closer, reaching out with a hand that hovered over the amulet, her fingers twitching as if resisting the urge to touch it.

"This amulet is no ordinary trinket," she murmured, her tone suddenly grave. "It's a tether—a piece of something larger. Destroying it won't be easy. And even if you succeed, you'll be left marked. Changed."

"We'll take the risk," Leena said firmly, her expression unwavering. "Just tell us how."

Mara's lips curved into a slow, unsettling smile. "Very well. But understand this: there is no half-measure. Once we begin, you'll be bound to the consequences of whatever emerges."

Rothar exchanged a glance with Leena, his face set with grim determination. "We're ready."

Mara stepped back, spreading her arms as she began to chant in a language that twisted through the air like smoke, each syllable heavy with power. The stones around them began to hum, vibrating with an energy that pulsed in time with the amulet in Rothar's pouch. He felt it grow warmer, a dark heat that seeped through the fabric, burning against his side.

"Place the amulet in the center," Mara instructed, her voice sharp, commanding.

Rothar hesitated, then pulled the amulet from his pouch, feeling the unsettling energy coiling around it like a serpent. He stepped forward, placing it in the center of the circle. The moment it touched the ground, the symbols on the stones flared, casting an eerie light across the clearing.

Mara's chant grew louder, more intense, the words weaving through the air like a binding spell. The amulet pulsed, the darkness within it roiling, fighting against the magic that surrounded it. Rothar felt a pressure building in his chest, as if the very air was thickening, suffocating him.

The ground trembled, a low rumble that sent ripples through the earth. The amulet began to crack, thin lines spidering across its surface, releasing wisps of black smoke that coiled upward, twisting and writhing like tendrils of shadow.

"Leena, prepare yourself!" Mara shouted, her eyes blazing as she directed her power toward the amulet. "It will fight back, and it will be ruthless."

Leena's face was pale, but her hands were steady as she raised her charm, channeling her own energy into the ritual. The blue light mingled with the dark tendrils, pushing back the shadow as it struggled to escape.

The amulet shattered, a final crack splitting it in two, and a surge of dark energy exploded from it, filling the clearing with a blinding light. Rothar staggered back, shielding his eyes, feeling the force of the explosion in his bones.

When the light faded, a figure stood where the amulet had been, a twisted, nightmarish shape cloaked in shadow, its eyes glowing like embers in the darkness. The Whispering One had emerged, a creature of pure malice and darkness, bound to the amulet no longer.

"You think you can destroy me?" it hissed, its voice like nails scraping against glass. "I am eternal. I will consume you."

Leena raised her charm, her face set with fierce determination. "You may be eternal, but you are not invincible."

The creature lunged toward her, its form shifting and warping as it moved, a mass of shadow and teeth and claws. Rothar leapt forward, his sword slicing through the air, meeting the creature with a force that sent a shockwave through his arms. The blade bit into the shadow, but it felt like slicing through smoke, each piece reforming as quickly as it was cut.

"Keep it distracted!" Mara shouted, her voice strained as she raised her hands, chanting a spell that wove through the air like a web, ensnaring the creature.

Leena's charm flared, a beam of blue light piercing the creature's form, searing through the darkness. It shrieked, recoiling, but it turned on her, its eyes blazing with fury. Rothar charged again, swinging his sword in a brutal arc that forced it back, each strike driving it closer to the edge of the circle.

"Now!" Mara cried, her voice ringing with power. She slammed her hands down, and the stones around them flared, casting a blinding light that engulfed the creature. The shadow writhed, shrieking as the light seared it, tearing it apart piece by piece.

Rothar held his breath, watching as the creature dissolved, its form breaking apart like smoke in the wind. The air grew still, the light fading as the last remnants of the shadow vanished, leaving only silence.

Leena staggered, catching herself against one of the stones, her face pale and drained. Rothar moved to her side, steadying her, his own breath ragged.

"It's done," Mara said quietly, her voice heavy with exhaustion. She turned to them, a faint smile on her lips. "The Whispering One is gone. But remember, the darkness it carried will leave scars."

Rothar nodded, his gaze drifting to the cracked ground where the amulet had lain. He felt the weight of her words, a reminder of the cost they had paid, the scars they would carry.

Leena looked up at him, her eyes reflecting the same exhaustion, the same weariness that he felt. But there was also a spark of determination, a silent promise that they would face whatever came next together.

As they turned to leave the clearing, the first rays of dawn broke through the trees, casting a warm, golden light over the forest. Rothar took one last look at the stones, feeling a sense of finality settle over him. They had survived the darkness, but he knew that HollowGate would always hold shadows.

And as long as it did, they would be there to face them.

Heroes Never Die
By: Chris Mason

"When you allow strength and
courage to reside in your heart,
there won't be room for fear or doubt.
Be strong. Be courageous. Have no
fear. Have no doubt."

Knight-General Renault Valoreign

Prologue

Within the rushing, crushing, twisting rapids, Miona fought for her life. However, the cold, relentless stings of the roaring cascade, combined with the weight of her armor, made the task nigh impossible as the oppressive waters forced her along the pit of the valley, threatening to devour her at any moment.

Yet she refused to give in. She tried focusing on her connection to the Holy light of the Faith to help heal the pain of her shattered arm, although the effort proved futile. She thrashed and kicked against the invisible hands of the current reaching up from beneath the water's surface to drag her to her watery grave.

The day had been full of fighting, and although exhausted, she wouldn't stop now. She spotted the roots of a nearby tree and tried to grab them. But the waves dipped, and before she could regain her bearings, her will was shattered as she slammed into the underwater stone lying in wait. Pain laced itself throughout her chest and stomach, the merciless sensation of having the wind snatched from her body.

Another chance presented itself as the top of another stone peeked above the foam of the cascading river. She steeled her resolve and reached out at the slab of rock. Her heart dropped as her fingertips scrapped against the granite surface, certain that she had missed her chance at salvation. She twisted her body and grasped once more before the moment was well beyond reach. Her hand found a shallow groove within the rock, and she dug as deeply into it as she could. Miona pulled herself onto the stone and coiled around the tiny island with what little strength remained.

However, the river seemed to acknowledge this defiance and surged with a much greater intensity, pulverizing Miona beyond what she could endure. Its roar drowned out Miona's cry for survival as each wall of water hammered away at her broken body, opening her wounds, and stealing her strength while adding to its own.

The stings of the water robbed Miona of her sight, tore her throat apart as it choked her shouts into an icy silence, and its deafening chorus filled her ears with its song of dominance. Finally, she felt the fingers of involuntary submission peel her fingers away from the stone in which she had found solace as the walls of her mind came under siege.

Relentlessly, the waves crashed against her repeatedly until her body surrendered to her unyielding foe. Her grip slipped, and the current claimed its prize as it snatched Miona away, twisting and tangling her even deeper beneath the water's surface.

Once more, through the chaos, through the pain, through the fear, and through uncertainty, she reached out with her heart and prayed.

As the light in her mind flickered, she held fast to her prayer. Her lungs burned and the world within her mind's eye spiraled away. Feeling left her body, and she gasped as the last of her breath fled her lungs.

The current spit Miona to the surface again where she was greeted with an unfortunately clear view of the sky. What were once beautiful, cerulean skies had become a pool the color of oxblood. Thick, white, clouds of cotton had grown absent, now replaced with black outlines of uncanny faces, glowering and tortured, watching the land and its people from above, screaming with thunderous blaspheme.

She crashed into another rock, splitting her helm. Her mind blacked and she floated like a stringless kite through an endless expanse, cold and dark. In this dark chasm of unconsciousness within her mind's eye, she drifted aimlessly and cried tears of pain, frustration, and anger.

That day had brought them all nothing but pain, dread, and loss. Nothing could've prepared Miona—or any of them—for what had occurred that day.

"Papa!" A child shouted.

The voice wasn't familiar. Miona awoke, disoriented, lying on the cold, wet earth.

Footsteps beat a steady rhythm as they rapidly approached.

"A survivor!" Miona heard a man shout as she was snatched out of the water by powerful hands.

Gold glinted in the mud near her. She recognized it in an instant.

It was the medallion that belonged to her mentor.

"Renault . . ." Miona muttered.

Where was he?

She reached for it, but her hand would not respond.

With what strength that remained, she rolled to face the bleeding sky where blood rained south of the Asphodel Mountains.

Miona gazed up at the churning crimson sky, her defeat a feast for the darkness above. The cold crept into her bones, tugging her toward oblivion, but something sparked in her chest—that old, familiar fire. An oath burned there still, unextinguished.

She felt its hatred bearing down, knew it yearned to extinguish her as it had the others. For as long as she would draw breath, hope would endure—and hope was the one thing the Black Star could not abide in its realm.

Part I

Seven Months Later

Miona bowed her head in prayer as shadows danced across the walls of her sparse bedroom in the flicker of the meager candlelight. Her armor, set upon its mount in a darkened corner, glittered in the meager light, keeping company her sacred Faith-blessed sword and shield.

Once her prayer was complete, Miona turned to the nightstand. The medallion she had held onto after all these fleeting months shone there in the delicate light. The edges of the sun etched in its center glowed softly and sent her heart to skip.

A Holy relic handed down from Knight-General to Knight-General within the Order of the First Light, the medallion still stole her breath.

She had no right to hold such divinity, nor even be in its presence, for she was no Knight-General. Not by a long shot. But fate had proclaimed the medallion, and the responsibility that it carries, be placed within her care.

The relic glinted, and suddenly Miona was back there—smoke thick in her lungs, steel ringing against steel.

"Miona!" Knight-General Renault's voice cut through the chaos. Through the haze, she saw Sister Laurel rising, armor still dripping crimson from her death wound. Laurel's eyes, once warm with kindness, now blazed with unnatural light. The sister who had trained beside her for years lunged with inhuman speed—claws aimed at Miona's throat. No final breath had passed Laurel's lips before darkness had laid its claim, turning her against her own.

"Miona."

The Paladin snapped from her trance, startled.

A young girl stood in the doorway, holding a tray of food in her hands.

"Hello, Maggie," Miona greeted with words full of warmth.

"I know you're leaving soon," Maggie said. Between teary sniffles, she added, "and I wanted to make you breakfast."

Miona smiled and took the tray. She knelt "Come, pray with me."

Maggie knelt as well, folding her hands and bowing her head.

Miona spoke softly, "Would you like to lead us in prayer?"

"Really?"

"Absolutely," Miona encouraged. "Just like how I taught you. From the heart."

After a moment of silence, Maggie went ahead with her words. "Precious light of the Faith that watches over us . . ." She opened an eye and looked up at Miona for approval and the woman smiled and nodded.

The girl continued. "Please take care of my friend, Miona. Please protect her and Lumen from the monsters. Oh, Lumen is her horse. He's really nice. If they ever get lost in the darkness, please light their way. If they ever get hungry, please give them something to eat, and . . ."

Her little voice warbled, and Miona leaned closer to her.

". . . After she saves the world, please help her find her way home. Light, bloom."

Miona and Maggie then said in unison, "and Faith walk with us."

The Paladin smiled down at the young girl, "Maggie, that was beautiful. Thank you so much for that."

"Of course," the little girl beamed. ". . . I'll miss you," Maggie whispered between sobs, fighting back her tears. She puffed up her chest and straightened her small shoulders, before bursting out, "I won't cry. I'm going to be brave like you."

"Being brave doesn't mean never crying," Miona said softly, pulling her close. "It means standing up again after the tears fall." She held Maggie until her trembling subsided.

"Please be careful, Miona. Oh, and..." Maggie unwound her tattered red scarf—the one she'd worn every day since Miona had first met her. "Take this. It's my lucky scarf."

Miona's throat tightened. "Oh, Maggie, I couldn't—"

"It's okay. I want you to take it." The young girl pressed it into her hands. "It's been good to me, and it'll be good to you. And..." The hope in Maggie's heart pushed a small smile to the surface. "When you're out there, it'll be like I'm there with you."

The scarf was still warm from the girl's neck as Miona wrapped it around her shoulders. She kneeled and touched her fist to her heart in the Paladin's salute, fighting back her own tears as the tiny girl mirrored the gesture with solemn determination.

After she left, Miona stared at the closed door, the scent of fresh bread rising from the tray. Such a small gift, that scarf. But it carried the weight of all she fought to protect.

After she completed another session of prayer, Miona fell into deeper silence. The time had come. She adjusted her borrowed armor one final time before mounting her horse, Lumen, who awaited her patiently outside. The bruises on her shoulders from Warren's iron grip still ached; a small price to pay for salvation from the river's fury all those months ago.

Townspeople lined the path to Stonewater's gates, their voices rising in prayer and farewell. She nodded to each familiar face, throat tight with words she couldn't voice. At the gates, Warren's broad shape emerged from the crowd.

"How's the armor?" He reached up to tap a pauldron with knuckles scarred by time and experience. "It fit good?"

Miona rolled her shoulders, testing the weight. "That it does," she affirmed. "It speaks well of your craft, Warren." She found that her voice was still a bit rough from lingering injuries. "Though

I wish . . ." She stopped, touching the warped holy seal she'd salvaged from her ruined Paladin plate.

"Aye, couldn't save the original." Warren's eyes softened, sensing the woman's somber tone. "That armor took the beating meant for you, though. And while these pieces weren't forged with holy hammers, they'll serve their purpose." He focused on Miona, giving her assurance with his words. "They'll keep you alive. That's holy enough for now."

Miona smiled and knocked her fist against the chest plate.

Warren grinned, but his voice faltered. "It seems like yesterday when you washed ashore here. Maggie was so worried about you; she stayed by your side the entire time. There were many times I didn't think you'd survive. I'm glad you proved me wrong."

Miona's heart trembled with tender emotions as she clutched the precious scarf, forever anchoring her heart to the village that had become her second home.

The town priest, Father Bernard, then joined Miona and Warren, carrying a small brown pouch in his hands. "And so, the hour of your departure has arrived. I'm sure that you don't need me to tell you about the perils ahead that you'll face during your journey to the Grand Spires. Because of the Black Star, the world you once knew has been twisted into something foreign and strange, growing more dangerous with every passing day."

What the priest said was true. The Black Star swelled in the reaches above them and so too did its influence over the Star-Scarred as well as the land itself.

"If the star continues to strengthen," Bernard went on, "I fear things will get much, much worse."

While Miona recovered in Stonewater, knights and soldiers from across the Cerulean Fields banded together to form raids to storm the Grand Spires where the entity gathered its energy from above.

But the raids never ventured beyond the gates of the city, and information about their where-abouts got choked and lost in the mist.

"However," the priest went on, "there is hope, because there is you. And as a Paladin of the First Light, you possess the gift of being able to commune with the Spirit of Holy Fire." He regarded the medallion at the center of Miona's chest piece.

Miona traced her fingers across the medallion, doubt crossing the ocean of her mind.

Whoever was worthy of carrying the medallion could speak with the spirit. But it had always been the Knights General. She was only a Knight of Grace, within their circle of Paladins. One day, she would make the journey to Sanctuary. Yet, a single thought consumed her . . .

Unworthy.

The word echoed with each heartbeat. She'd watched her brothers and sisters fall, one by one. Their blood stained her dreams, their faces haunted her in rain puddles that she'd pass, and now their empty armor lined the halls of her memory—a gallery of her failures. No. She was not worthy. She found absurdity in the mere thought. She was no Renault . . .

"Before you confront the end of the world," he said, his voice drawn in an ominous, almost threatening tone. He hesitated, letting the weight of his words press down over her, then continued, ". . . journey westward to Sanctuary and earn the favor of the Spirit of Holy Fire. Only with its Flames of Retribution will you be able to turn the enemies of light into ash. But be wary: the Black Star's minions know you are alive, and they fear what the survival of the Order of the First Light means. Our future, and their end, walks with you. They will dispatch their hordes upon you, unleashing their all to prevent you from gaining the weapon that can undo their schemes."

He handed Miona the small pouch. "I have charged these crystals with the Holy power of the Faith through prayer. Keep them close to you, sister," he said. "If, by chance, that you require more, my protégé, Titus, has been traveling throughout the Fields with his allies, searching for survivors. Please keep a watch out for him."

As she took the bag, Miona could feel the warmth of the crystals inside, as well as the weight of everyone's hopes and dreams. "Thank you, Bernard," she smiled. "For everything."

The priest continued, "The road ahead is perilous, and despair will descend upon you. But in times of fear, in times of uncertainty, I ask that you reflect on prayers you've made and prayers you've answered. And know that the Faith moves through all things. Trust and know this, Sister Miona, for it will always be your guiding light."

He bowed. "Light bloom and Faith walk with you." She saluted Bernard and Warren with the gesture of Faith's Fanfare, once again placing her open palm over the center of her chest.

Miona and her trusted steed, Lumen, took their first steps into the strange new world beyond the open gates of Stonewater, each one heavy, but growing lighter with determination. The protective light of their refuge faded behind them as horse and rider entered the Cerulean Fields once more.

Seven months had passed since she had last set foot into the fields. She recalled blue skies and ivory-colored clouds cast soft shadows across rolling green hills. Trees burgeoning with juicy fruit and the colorful birds singing and twittering in their branches dotted the landscape, and the soft babbling of crystalline streams brought life to the land.

Now, the icy air raised gooseflesh on her arm as flakes of gray snow swirled about as she watched a rotting vulture return her gaze. Skies the color of dried blood and black clouds like scabs against festering wounds, cast moving shadows where strange horrors lurked within. Fields of bone and rotting flesh filled the air with a pungent odor that burned her eyes and nose. The trees were wrong, made of flesh, their branches resembling the arms of monsters she had only read about before in scripture. Instead of the babbling of crystalline streams, dull slaps of thick, black liquid bubbled and belched as it gurgled along the old river bed.

Miona's heart raced with heartbreak. as beautiful memories battled with reality. She could not. She would not accept it. This was no place for fantasy—oblivion had ridden the light of the stars to their home and corrupted their world.

"Dearest Cerulean," she uttered, "What have they done to you?"

It only took a single season for the lands of the Cerulean Fields to fall underneath the glare of the crimson light that had transformed the sacred land into a sprawling hellscape infested with dangerous, bizarre creatures.

Plagues, indiscriminate to humans or nature, spread like wrathful wildfires. No healer understood their cause, and no sage possessed the knowledge of a cure.

In their feverish state, those inflicted by the sickness spoke of a voice that whispered to them from above. As the illness progressed, the afflicted were seen staring upwards for sustained periods of time without eating, sleeping, or even blinking while uttering unintelligible nonsense.

However, there was one ominous, intelligible phrase spoken by them all.

"No one is lost. All are found. The Black Star beckons."

The scars that would form caused the inflicted to claw at their eyes in feverish madness, desperate to see the Black Star in all its unholy glory, giving birth to the illness' name, "The Star-Scarred Plague."

And then, the afflicted vanished, leaving behind friends and family, hearts aching and filled with questions.

The mist came at midnight, black as pitch and hungry. Claws scraped stone in its depths, and Eastern Cerulean's towns fell one by one, leaving only silence and ash in their wake.

The militia and town guards fought to protect the citizens, but didn't stand a chance against the horde that lurked within the mist. Men and women took to arms and stood shoulder to shoulder against their foes and met them head on. Sounds of a battle could be heard from within the blanket of fog, but the agents of darkness were not the ones to fall. The screams of Cerulean's protectors faded one by one as steel bent and wood splintered as the monsters tore through the armed forces, leaving them as mismatched pieces on the ground. Behind locked doors, families watched their loved ones, now sick, twisted, and robbed of their own will, stumble home, faces twisted, eyes vacant. Hands that once offered comfort now destroyed homes and tore flesh from bone. From house to house, village by village, the evil tide didn't yield until it had swept across the whole of the Cerulean Fields.

Miona's shoulders and chest heaved as fury washed over her, drowning out her fears. She refused the unnatural world around here, making a promise to it, her people, and herself that she would return the sacred light of the Faith to the beautiful lands she once knew, and she knew that she would sacrifice any and everything to make it so, no matter the cost.

She grazed her fingertips across the medallion embedded in the center of her chest plate and recalled Renault's return from Sanctuary.

Before the monsters reached the Grand Spires, Renault vanished to the Holy ground. When he returned days later, light seemed to bend around him, and the air crackled in his wake. Even the temple stones hummed in his presence. As his Paladins stood near him, they all exchanged whispers and glances as the warmth of his light washed across their skin. Whatever blessing the Knight-General had received on that sacred ground made him burn like a living flame.

The Order of the First Light stood taller that day, shields gleaming, blades sharp, faith unshakable. With Renault's holy fire to guide them, victory felt certain.

But faith alone couldn't stop the darkness. And now, watching the corrupted sky, Miona wondered how many prayers it would have taken to change their fate. What mortal preparation could have readied them for the end of all things?

Clutching the medallion, Miona breathed deeply, steadying herself in meditation. "Lumen," she said, peering over the landscape, "To business!" She shouted and spurred Lumen into a gallop across the cursed lands toward Sanctuary.

The coarse, frigid air whipped around her face. Something caught in her throat—bitter and acrid. She coughed, tasting char on her tongue. What she'd taken for snow was ash—another sign of her dying world to add to so much more. She pulled Maggie's scarf upon the bridge of her nose for protection from the cold as well as the toxic flakes and leaned against Lumen.

They pressed on.

They passed smoldering craters filled with charred corpses that littered the countryside. Silhouettes of colossal skeletons roamed the wastelands at the edge of her eyesight, their gargantuan skulls lit by the ominous glow of the Star-Scarred.

Lumen veered from the path as crimson mist pooled in the valley below, the writhing shadows and Star-Scarred eyes within proving Lumen and Miona shared instincts.

Broken buildings jutted against the horizon like demonic teeth. Miona's vision blurred, her arms heavy from hours of fighting the wind and rugged terrain. Even Lumen's steps had grown uneven, stumbling on loose stones. The setting sun promised only deeper shadows ahead. They needed shelter, no matter how desperate the ruins looked.

After a cursory search of the town, Miona spotted a standing stable that offered decent shelter and a bundle of soft straw to rest against. Before she allowed herself to rest, she whispered a prayer of protection. "Precious Faith, thank you for your blessed light. I ask that you please give us protection against our enemies as we sleep." There was a flash of light in response to her words and the ground underneath her feet hummed with soft illumination.

The presence of the Faith fell onto Miona's spirit like a singular, gentle ray of sunlight. With the promise of protection over her and her companion, and despite the glowing, stalking eyes of the vulture which had yet to release its gaze from her ever since she ventured into the Fields, Miona drifted into slumber.

An icy shriek woke Miona from a troubled sleep. She jolted up, heart pounding in her chest, hand grasping the hilt of her nearby sword. Another piercing scream—the voice filled with fear, pleading for help.

Miona muttered a swift prayer for safety, and snatched up her healing kit, cinched up her sword belt, grabbed her shield, and rushed outside the barn. Anyone still alive in this hellscape would be desperate indeed, and likely pursued by the hungry, mindless Star-Scarred.

Through the gloom, she spotted a woman fleeing toward a crumbling inn, dark shapes in pursuit. Her oath burned in her chest as she drew steel and followed.

A quick look told Miona the lower floor was abandoned and footprints, wet from the sickly landscape, led to a dilapidated staircase. She rushed upstairs. The prints led to a landing, then through a long hall, to a door at the end. She padded forward, leading with her shield. Her eyes fixed ahead, relying only on her peripheral vision to detect other enemies, she passed wooden support beams and banisters on one side of the hall, and several broken doorways to the left and right—rooms, now in disrepair, dark and silent.

She pushed open the door at the end.

A woman, knees pulled to her chest, huddled in the corner, dark hair covering her face.

Where were the Scarred?

Miona rushed to her side. The woman's face snapped up at her, hair falling away. Her face was wrong. Her eyes, set deep in dark pits, were wide, round, and wild—all wrong. Dried blood—or some other black substance—lined the sides of her mouth. Miona stifled a gag reflex as a pungent odor wafted from the woman's mouth.

The woman spoke, her voice a twisted, unworldly sound. "Oh . . . you're so brave . . . and so very stupid."

A trap. The woman was bait.

Three men rose—black shadows bearing steel—from the darkened door behind her.

How had she been so stupid? So unfocused?

It had been months since Miona had seen combat, and her instincts were clearly off. But she had at least practiced and kept her blade-and-shield skills sharp while recuperating.

The first ambusher lunged forth, thrusting a dingy knife at Miona's flank. The Paladin easily sidestepped the attack, and the blade sliced only air. She delivered a swift, stiff backhand to the bandit, smashing his face with her shield.

He tumbled backward. Another foe erupted into the room, taking his place. This one brandished a short sword, dull but still deadly. He swung, his attacks sloppy and wild.

The seasoned Holy knight didn't bother to parry the inexperienced attacks, easily sidestepping the blade.

The attacker bellowed in frustration as every slash failed to connect, each slash growing wilder and more desperate than the last. Miona saw her opening and countered. She snatched the man's wrist and twisted. He cried out as his shoulder went sideways and dropped his weapon.

Miona's back was now toward the door.

The third foe pushed into the room behind her. He slammed his fist into the side of her head, sending her ears ringing and momentarily stunning her. The attacker didn't hesitate. He threw his arms around her in a bear hug and pulled her in.

The sword-wielding enemy retrieved his weapon, still nursing his shoulder, and approached more carefully now from the front.

She shook off the ringing and slammed her head into the face of the man grasping her. Once. Twice. Three times. He grunted and fell back, still maintaining his grip. She pressed backwards against him to keep him off balance and built distance with her frontal attacker.

They stumbled back into the hallway, where the first attacker that she had downed was still stunned and sprawled across the ground.

Backpedaling hard, Miona took advantage of her momentum and kicked him in the face with the heel of her steel boot, sending blood and teeth spattering onto the floor.

She reset her heel into the wooden planks, and, with a final push, bent her knees and lunged backward, hammering her captor into a wooden support beam.

The man grunted, blowing the wind from him. Gasping, his arms fell, and he bent forward, sucking painful air.

Miona spun on her heel and slammed her pommel into his forehead. He toppled forward, and she delivered a full-frontal kick, knocking him stumbling back through the balcony to crash onto the first floor.

The sword-wielder rushed toward Miona's back and took another wild swing. But she'd expected the undisciplined strike. She spun and ducked the wide swipe and shouldered his gut. Leveraging herself under him, she flipped him over her head, sending him screaming over the banister to crash into the floor below with his companion.

One left to finish.

The final enemy, dazed, struggled back onto his knees, his back to the paladin. Miona took a quick breath before stomping the back of his leg and slammed her shield into the back of his head. He collapsed on the floor.

Finally, she turned her attention back to the bait and smirked. "Looks like you're next," she said and waved the woman forward with her sword. "Come on."

"Stay back!" The woman shouted as she brandished a pitiful knife she'd produced from somewhere in her rags.

The first droplet hit the windowsill like spilled wine. Outside, red fluid spattered the walls, thick as blood. The Breath of the Black Star oozed through the town like a kraken's tentacles, probing every shadow, hungry, ever devouring.

The bait's eyes fixed on the crimson mist. Her breath hitched at the guttural whispers from the street, and panic set in. Her fingers clawed at her skirts, legs tensing to bolt. "No, no, no . . ." The whisper built with each ragged breath until Miona's gauntleted hand clamped over her mouth, pulling her back into the shadows as the chant from the evil parade grew louder.

"No one is lost. All are found. The Black Star beckons."

"No one is lost. All are found. The Black Star beckons."

"No one is lost. All are found. The Black Star .
. ."

A horde of Star-Scarred monstrosities surged into the inn's rotted doors. Before the two ambushers could rise, the shadow-mob consumed them. The thralls' chanting rose with each spray of crimson blood, their mantra drowning out the men's last screams.

Miona held the woman against her, forcing them both to stillness as the frenzy continued below. When silence finally fell, only a dark stain remained where the bandits had been, and the creatures drifted back to their vacant-eyed state and drifted listlessly from the building.

Miona slowly peeled her hand from the woman's mouth.

The surviving bandit, lost in her own shock and grief, screamed from her soul at the loss of her comrades.

This drew the attention of the thralls back into the inn where they were driven into a frenzy at the sight of Miona.

She knocked the bait woman away from the balcony into safety as she took sword and shield to arms.

Miona's shield smashed the first thrall down the stairs. More clawed up through the broken balcony—too many. She leapt down, drawing them away from the cowering woman above.

Steel flashed. Bodies fell. But they kept coming as Miona's sword arm grew heavier, her lungs burning. When hands seized her armor, she couldn't break free. They slammed her to the plank floor.

She slashed wildly, kicking, fighting the press of cold flesh. She resigned herself to die here in this place . . . it was a good death . . .but her mission had failed.... She uttered a prayer of forgiveness. Of absolution and—

A brief flicker of silver light appeared and plummeted from above. Yellow light exploded through the fog, and the thralls recoiled, stunned.

The consecrated power of Faith called from the heavens—she knew that holy glow.

Her prayer had been answered.

Then a great sword swept through the night, cleaving the remaining thralls in two as the fading Faith-fire lit the street, turning the monsters to torches.

An armored hand thrusted down to her. "Are you alright?"

Miona hesitated before clasping it, muscles screaming as she rose. Three figures materialized from the gloom—the man who helped her up, a swordsman in battered plate, his claymore dark with thrall blood. Behind him, a mage in travel-worn robes waited in the shadows, one hand plunged into her robes, the other gripping her staff. Her eyes narrowed as she regarded Miona. The third remained half-hidden, watching.

No crests that she could see. No holy symbols. Yet they'd wielded the powers of Faith and flame against the darkness. Before she could question them—

"That medallion!" The watcher's voice cracked with recognition. "You're . . . you're from the Order of the First Light! Who are you?" Asked the young watcher from the shadows. His voice held not a little tinge of accusation.

She puffed her chest out, slipped her sword into its scabbard, and met the young man's eyes, her own indignation rising. "My name is Miona Dawnbrighton, Knight of Grace of the Order of the First Light."

The young warrior spoke, "My Lady. My name is Titus Alero. Priest from the Town of Stonewater to the East. This is Stormson Steiner and Dustevei Darrowmere." He regarded the warrior and mage respectively.

"Titus of Stonewater?" Miona said, instantly making the connection. "Father Bernard spoke of you."

Titus's eyes widened with joy. "You know him?"

Miona nodded, "Yes. I spent time there, recovering from a battle many months ago. He prayed with me, and for me, for countless hours. I am beyond grateful for him. He told me that our paths may cross, yours and mine."

"A Paladin from the Order of the First Light," Dustevei's voice caught. "It's not possible. Reports said that they were massacred."

"Yet she bears the Medallion of the Knight-General," The young priest rasped out.

Stormson's eyes fixed on the sacred emblems of Miona's sword and shield. "And what looks to be Faith-blessed steel. Seems like First Light to me."

"Or a corpse-robber," Dustevei cut in, fingers squeezing her staff.

Stormson replied, "Faith-blessed weapons burn any unworthy hand."

The mage scoffed. "Then it's a replica. Nothing more."

Stormson held out a hand. "May I prove a point to my overly cautious friend?"

Miona obliged and held the hilt of her sword out to the large man who took hold of the weapon. Before any of them could even blink, a searing hot pain burned the warrior's skin, and he gratefully handed the blade back to its owner.

"It's quite real," Stormson said, waving his hand to soothe the burn.

Dustevei refused to discard her skepticism.

Titus' eyes shimmered. "A Paladin of the First Light. I knew the Faith wouldn't abandon us."

The mage scoffed again. "Excuse me? Look around you. The Faith has long since abandoned this place."

"As long as we live, Faith remains. If you didn't have hope, then what are you fighting for? Why keep going?" Titus replied.

Dustevei turned away. "I tire of this endless jabbering. I'm going to look for survivors and supplies. Have you seen anyone, Paladin?"

"There's a woman in the inn there. Her comrades were consumed by Star-Scarred."

Dustevei took her leave.

"Why don't you join us? We're stronger together," Stormson offered.

Miona touched her medallion. "Much appreciated. But I must go alone." Her voice softened. "I've seen what happens to those who stand too close."

Titus glanced at Stormson, nodding. "Brother, your healing potions. I sense the Faith at work within her, but she lacks potent healing powers. She needs them more than we."

Stormson pulled two vials from his armor. "All yours, Miona."

"Faith guides your heart, Paladin," Titus added, offering Faith's Fanfare salute. "The darkness has taken much, but seeing you gives me hope. May Faith walk with you."

Miona returned the salute, grateful for this small mercy. "And with you."

She returned to the barn where her companion awaited her return, protected from the Star-Scarred. There, she mounted Lumen, the potions secure in her saddlebags—gifts she prayed would save another's life, if not her own.

A thin, pale light battled to pierce the noxious blanket of red and black clouds, reaching into the dark heavens beyond the twisted, cursed wasteland; its faint glow barely visible in the distance, offering a fragile hope against the suffocating darkness.

Miona could not suppress a hopeful smile. But a cacophony of tortured wails that clawed at her sanity harbinger a mob of twisted figures, their limbs contorted and skeletal, scrambling madly toward her from the ruined, ash-strewn lands washed her rising hope—and her smile—away.

The curse that corrupted the land seemed to know the Paladin's intentions—and put forth its hand to stop her.

Lumen, sensing the land's fate rested on his shoulders, ran like the wind, the oppressive, dark sky, a menacing presence above.

These Star-Scarred humans, exposed to the Black Star's corrupting influence far longer than those Miona had encountered so far, bore the mark of its foul power in their twisted forms and glowing eyes. As the Star-Scarred Hunters closed the distance, their twisted forms, more powerful than any human, reached out with writhing tentacles; their guttural growls echoed through the air as they ran on their haunches. A red mist, like a foul exhalation, sparked from their hunched, corrupt forms, the air heavy with the stench of decay and malice emanating from their bodies. Gaping jaws, impossibly wide, revealed rows of jagged fangs that flashed in the dark. Their numbers seemed to have no end. Three beasts became six. Six became twelve. Then twelve became more than she could count.

Miona, clinging to her steed as it galloped, felt the strengthening wind buffet her face, the brightening light beyond the hill a stark contrast to the deepening shadows behind them.

The speed of the creatures was uncanny and swiftly closed the distance between themselves and their prey.

As they made the final turn, Miona spied a wall of light that reached into the sky, higher than she could see. But her heart skipped a beat when she felt Lumen stagger in his steps, exhaustion demanding its debt to be paid.

The creatures leapt at the Paladin and her steed, their quarry finally within reach.

However, the monsters quickly turned into ash as a wave of golden fire flared from the wall, leaving the Paladin and her mount intact.

A fiery, golden light engulfed the golden building of The Sanctuary of Holy Fire. The structure was enormous. The light it emitted was bright and warm. The monsters that had been on her heels dared not tread on the hallowed ground and stood just outside of the ring of light that radiated from the building itself.

No longer able to walk, or even stand, Lumen slowed to a trot before collapsing to the ground, heaving for air. Miona knelt on the horse and stroked his face lovingly before standing and making her way to the colossal front doors of the Holy building.

The two titanic doors, imposing and dark, stood centered between four massive stone columns, etched with ancient symbols. The empty circular slot at the base of the doors seemed to silently beckon. The medallion in Miona's chest plate vibrated, humming with a low thrum that grew louder as she approached the door; a warm light emanated from it as she removed it and carefully slotted it into place.

Glowing runes, etched into the medallion, pulsed with light, their patterns climbing the doors in a mesmerizing dance of light and shadow. The doors parted, releasing a wave of shimmering, golden light that seared the Paladin's eyes.

But as the golden light faded, she found herself breathless, gazing at amber clouds ablaze against a sunset-colored sky, tiny gold sparkles drifting around her like ethereal snowflakes. Crystal clear water flowed underneath her feet as she watched the river from above as if she stood on solid air. Before her, a honey-colored stairway ascended into the clouds.

Again, the medallion pulsed within her armor, its light a warm gold against her chest, mirroring the rhythmic thrumming of the stairway before her. As she placed her foot on the first step, the clouds parted, revealing a stairway that seemed to stretch into infinity.

The climb felt endless; days blurred into one another as she ascended, finally reaching the final step. A glowing waterfall was there, glistening with an ethereal light, cascaded into a pool at Miona's feet, the water radiating warmth from a place beyond the heavens. The air shimmered with heat.

Small sparks, like tiny fireflies, lifted from the pool, snapping and crackling in the air with a faint smell of ozone. After a while, their numbers swelled to an uncountable multitude, and the pool's waters shimmered like waves of gentle, dancing fire. From the silent, intensely bright blaze, a humanoid figure of pure light emerged, its back trailing flames like wings of the sun.

It spoke in a language unlike any Miona had ever heard, echoing with the weight of ages past, a time before time itself. Though the ancient entity's words were unintelligible, their resonance echoed in the medallion, its images painting a clear picture in her mind.

"Upholder of Light, Vessel of Order, and Instrument of Righteousness," the entity spoke, its wispy, ethereal form pulsing in golden light before the Paladin, "I know why you have come. The world is in chaos, its children struggle to find the light in the end times. Yet, their prayers have not fallen upon deaf ears, and they shall not go unanswered."

The entity closed on Miona, the Paladin's eyes reflecting the flames of the figure that stood before her.

"I can see the meditations of your heart," it said. "Your faith is unwavering. Despite everything that you have seen, everything that you have endured, and even in the uncertainty that lies ahead, you hold fast to your beliefs."

Miona nodded at every word, the fiery spirit reading the resolve in her dark brown eyes.

"If you believe that your cause is just," the spirit went on, "then you must be prepared to sacrifice everything that you hold true, everything that you are. Are you ready to bring your all to bear?"

Miona knelt at the edge of the waters, her voice barely a whisper. "I am unworthy. Others fought harder, believed deeper, stayed truer to their oaths. Why am I the one who lives?"

The spirit's flames danced across the water. "Step into the pool and accept this blessing."

Her hands trembled as she rose. Every fallen brother and sister's face flashed through her mind—their faith had been perfect, unshakeable. Yet here she stood, doubt heavy in her heart. But wasn't doubt itself an opportunity to strengthen her faith? To question, yet still step forward?

The fiery lake roared as she entered, each step a prayer, a confession, a promise. The waters sang with holy fury, scouring away her mortal fears until only faith remained. At the pool's heart, the spirit's touch ignited her soul—divine fire flooding every shadow of unworthiness until she blazed brighter than the sun itself, transformed by righteous flame into something both more and less than she had been.

Her voice, when it came, rang with both power and humility. "I accept this blessing not because I am worthy, but because I must be."

As the bright fog dissipated, the light faded, leaving her in the stillness of normal water, the only sound the gentle ripple of the current. Miona opened her eyes; a breath of golden fog, warm and soft, rolled out from within them.

Then, the spirit spoke to her, "Fly to the brink of this world's end, and scatter despair with righteous fire, leaving salvation and hope in its wake. But first, the creatures that sought to vanquish and devour your light, show them all what it means to stand on Holy ground."

Within a blink, Miona found herself outside of the Sanctuary, now devoid of light. She didn't question its absence; she knew its light now resided within her.

As she stepped back outside, Miona recognized the strange carrion bird which flew overhead. "That vulture ..." She watched it perch on the barren branch of a nearby tree. Her eyes were then drawn by a presence beneath the grotesque bird.

"Greetings, Paladin," the man spoke in deep, proper voice. "I am Zevraxes."

Before Miona sat an exceedingly thin man, his face shrouded by a hood, long, thick tattered ashen robes hanging from his frame.

He pointed at Miona. "I journeyed here to take your life."

By now, Lumen had cowered behind his rider, and Miona calmed him, urging him to stay back as she approached the cloaked figure. "You've been watching me," she said to the man, regarding his winged watcher.

Zevraxes nodded, the dim glow of his eyes seen from underneath his hood. "Indeed. There had been whisperings of a survivor from that day."

As the man spoke of the event, another memory triggered in Miona's mind.

Amid fighting against the tide of undead monstrosities underneath the shadows of her home, flashes of a ghastly emerald green illuminated within the fog whenever she witnessed a fallen comrade being raised to undeath on the battlefield. In this moment, she recognized the same glow in this man's face.

"You were there," Miona muttered. "The Necromancer that twisted my brothers and sisters, raising them into undeath."

"In the flesh," he said proudly. "Well, what's left of it, that is." He gave himself over to a self-gratifying chuckle. "There is belief that you threaten our Master's arrival." Zevraxes gestured to the sparking knot of bleeding clouds that hung over the silhouette of the spires in the distance. "But to be honest with you, that matters to me not. Your survival only means that I have failed my task. And I take my tasks very seriously."

Green light flared in his sunken eyes. The earth cracked, disgorging four armored corpses, emerald flame flickering in their hollow sockets.

The Paladin walked toward them and unsheathed her sword, the Awakened Clarity, with all the shades of living fire dancing along the runes which were now present across the weapon's face.

Miona pulled back her weapon, the sparks trailing behind like glittering embers. Within the next several heartbeats, the sparks grew into brilliant flickers of flames, crackling and spitting, before converging into a magnificent flare that illuminated the night. Then, the flare sang out in a deafening roar, a fiery shout of jubilation, the sound echoing through the night.

A power rose in her like a fire unchecked and flew from her mouth in a shout that shook the world to its foundation. She slashed with her fiery sword. Heat and sacred energy radiated off the blade, engulfing the undead and the Necromancer in a wave of fire and a lingering smell of sulfur. While Zevraxes was unharmed, all that was left of his minions was ash, swirling and carried away on the desolate wind.

The Necromancer scoffed. "So, you have been bestowed with the Holy Fire of the Faith. Your predecessor, Renault Valoreign, was one of the greatest Paladins that the Cerulean Fields had ever seen. On the day that your Order died, he wielded the flames as well. But he couldn't protect this precious land that he loved, he couldn't protect his Order, and he couldn't protect himself. In the end, the blessing meant nothing. He was nothing. The men and women of your Order died screaming and weeping in pain. The children of the Grand Spires put up a better struggle."

Hot tears welled in Miona's eyes and her teeth flashed and clenched at the blatant disrespect of her people. Zevraxes fed on the Paladin's rage and stoked her flames further.

"They were *nothing*? YOU are *nothing*."

Movement flickered behind her. Two more undead lunged as Miona dropped into a crouch, their blades scraping harmlessly across her shield. She pivoted, holy flame erupting from her sword as she cleaved through corrupted flesh.

More came, their unholy shrieks piercing the air. She met them blade for blade, each strike burning away the darkness that animated them. Zevraxes watched his soldiers fall, a thin smile spreading beneath his hood.

"Hmm. Careful, you're impressing me." He raised skeletal fingers. "But raw power didn't save your Order then, and it won't save you now. Behold."

The ground trembled. Pebbles tap danced at her feet as horror after horror clawed free of the earth. Giant skeletons hefted tree-sized clubs on the hills above. Rusted blades gleamed in the hands of fallen knights. Six-legged beasts prowled forward, their split maws revealing endless rows of teeth.

Miona lifted her blade, its holy light a star against the gathering dark.

Holy fire erupted from the blade, searing the undead ranks. "Is this it? Is this all that you command?!" She shouted as a ring of sacred flame spread outward. "You dare speak ill of the

Knight-General? You dare speak ill of my brothers and sisters? You dare speak ill of my home? You took EVERYTHING from us!"

The Paladin's rage was untethered, vast and boundless.

"I'LL KILL YOU!" Miona's roar spilled as another wave of furious fire that washed over more undead.

For just a moment, fear flashed in Zevraxes' glowing eyes. The monsters recoiled, burrowing back into the earth as if burned by her mere presence.

"Oh dear." His casual tone betrayed by the tension in his shoulders. "It seems our time is up. But congratulations—you've passed the test. Consider me intrigued."

Miona kept her blade raised, its glow reflecting off his skull-like features. "Save your games. Run. Tell your master that I'm coming for him. Him, you, and everything, in between. When you and I meet again, and we will, I'll show you all what true power is."

"True power to go along with that vengeful heart of yours. You know, we may not be so different after all. I'll tell my Lord you . . . simply got away." He leaned forward on his skeletal mount, masking retreat as mercy. "Grow stronger for me, little lioness. I await what comes at journey's end."

Green light cracked reality like breaking glass. "Until we meet again beneath the spires of your fallen home."

The portal shattered behind him, leaving only sparks and questions. Miona sheathed her sword, knowing her power had forced his hand. Her quest couldn't wait.

Lumen emerged from hiding, ready to carry her onward.

The Grand Spires rose before them, twisted monuments against the corrupted sky. Above, the Black Star pulsed like a festering wound, its dark crown crackling over her fallen home.

Miona touched Maggie's scarf at her neck, then the holy seal on her chest. Every step had led here—every loss, every battle, every prayer. The darkness thought it had won, thought it had broken the last Paladin.

Her blade ignited with sacred flame, and she smiled. Let it come.

Faith, after all, burned brightest in the dark.

About the Authors

Michael Magistro

Michael Magistro is a Clovis, California-based author with deep roots in the vibrant Bay Area. When not managing regional operations for a Fortune 150 company, Michael channels his passion into crafting compelling narratives that explore themes of redemption, legacy, rebirth, and the enduring search for hope in the darkest of times. Outside of his professional and creative pursuits, he enjoys powerlifting, devouring a wide range of media, and cherishing moments with his family.

James Andrews

James Andrews is a full time artist and designer living in the Northeastern United States. This is the first step in his journey as an author and he has many more stories to tell. When he's not sculpting dragons, drawing comics, or writing, he spends all the rest of his time with his golden retriever and his cat.

W.E. Wertenberger

W. E. Wertenberger is a writer of Sci-Fi, Fantasy and Crime fiction. He grew up in Northern Ohio and currently lives and works in Kentucky. His most recent work has appeared in Savage Realms Monthly and Cirsova Magazine.

Rob D. Smith

Rob D. Smith wanted to weave tales as soon as he plucked his first Fantastic Four comic book off the grocery store spinner rack. He honed his imagination with scribbled drawings in notebooks creating intricate stories where he learned that his imagination was far greater than his art skills. Words became his way of exploring the weird worlds in his mind. Since then, he has had wide success in the crime, horror, fantasy, and weird fiction genres.

Jack Finn

Jack Finn is a folk horror author and member of the Horror Writers Association. He lives in the Pacific Northwest with his wife and two clever dogs. His debut novel, The Seven Deaths of Prince Vlad (Anuci Press, 2024), explores dark and thrilling themes. In 2025, Jack's werewolf duology—Prey Upon the Lambs (April) and The Desolation of Hunters (September)—will be released by Anuci Press, along with They Come When You Are Asleep, an anthology of his short stories (Velox Books). His work has appeared in notable horror collections, including Doors of Darkness, Horroscope 4, Twelve Months of Horror, and more.

JP Wilder

JP Wilder, also known as JP Vile, is a versatile author and academic specializing in fantasy, science fiction, and pulp genres. Best known for his Crusader series and Hunter Caine Pulp Stories, Wilder delves into themes of war, honor, betrayal, and redemption through action-packed storytelling. He has contributed essays and introductions to the Edge Weaver Classics series, covering iconic works like A Princess of Mars and 20,000 Leagues Under the Sea. Wilder also explores historical mysteries and survival strategies in his academic works. Holding an MBA and an MFA in Creative Writing, he enriches his narratives with profound historical depth.

Chris Mason

Chris Mason is a fantasy and sci fi writer hailing from Jackson, Mississippi. He is the author of The Stars Fell (Science Fiction), as well as The Dark Rider (Dark Fantasy). A fan of epic storytelling centered around good versus evil, he can usually be found gaming on his couch with his cats, Quincy and Rocky, or traveling in search of new inspiration.